DUALITY AND DEATH

By George Jobb

Introduction

The story revolves around the main character Max Jobber, a mechanic by trade who was recruited into a group that called themselves "The Collectors". They could be described vigilantes that worked outside the justice system. However, they were more than that, they were part of a society that had operated for thousands of years. If it were oversimplified, they would only be washing shit off the sidewalk. What they were on a cosmic level, they are akin to gardeners, taking care of the people and the planets that they existed on. At some point they began to realize that there were portals that gave them access to alternate realities and species. One of the more benevolent entities of the group, is a woman named Elizabeth. She has been a gardener for centuries.

The premise of this story was loosely based on a conversation I had with retired city worker that was a friend of our family 30 years ago. The discussion came up on crime and punishment. With a weary look in his eyes he said that in the forties and fifties in British Columbia, that when they had a problem in town that wasn't going away, they would bring in a member of the policeman department from an adjoining community. The problem person would be removed and never seen if again.

The character Khon is loosely based on an interview done by Ross Kemp on YouTube of an East Indian sex trafficker who had claimed to of murdered between four and five hundred girls or women over a 7-year period.

In the last two chapters the reference to rebar distributed by Chinese companies through the world being contaminated with radioactive material is loosely based on a conversation I had with I retired engineering consultant. He had been hired short term to give an opinion on why the Vancouver airport foundations and concrete were generating heat and an electrical current.

Excerpt one

Dana Basham would be considered a very moderate Muslim from the people who knew him, they might not even know he was a Muslim. After seeing his own family and people of other ethnic groups murdered in his home country as a child. He had taken an oath to himself to protect all. He felt honored when Sam had approached him asking if he had an interest in contributing to society on a much deeper level. A level most people don't have the stomach or character for, without ever receiving recognition or financial reward.

Excerpt two

With a population of 1.2 billion it wasn't hard to hide things when you spread money around. If money wasn't enough of an incentive, then they were threatened. Both their livelihood and their families. What Chan was getting whispers of, was that the spent uranium rods from the nuclear reactors that were supposed to be going into deep underground storage in central China weren't. The rods were being cut into small pieces and added to large vats of molten steel used to make rebar. They were then sprayed with what was supposed to be a rust inhibitor, but in fact just prevented detection of radioactive material for several years. The rebar was then shipped overseas to foreign countries throughout the world at a discounted price to be used in construction.

This is a work of fiction, Names, characters, places and incidents are the author's imagination or are used fictitiously. Any resemblance to actual events, locales, or persons, living or dead, is entirely coincidental.

CHAPTER 1

The mechanic shop was always slow in January. The cold brick walls wet with condensation, blackened with grease, never seemed to heat up. It felt cave-ish, primitive. Max Jobber and the boys sat around the propane fueled heat lamp. Nobody had much to say, and they needed something to keep themselves engaged. Max would pick up a hobby vehicle, maybe a motorcycle to do repairs on over the slow months of winter. He had decided on a 1994 BMW K100 this year. He had seen a few of them stripped down and converted into Scramblers. These motorbikes have some clean lines, the type of bike one could take off road in the Pacific Northwest. This particular 1994 BMW K100 hadn't been run in a while. The previous owner assured him that it ran fine, but it had been a couple of years since. It only had 34,000 km on it, it wasn't unusual for those bikes to get over 150,000 kilometers on the original drivetrain. A new battery and a little TLC will put some life into it. Reliability, ease of maintenance and accessibility two parts have been built into these bikes. Using his hands for something other than violence helped him relax

I had saved a few photos over the last few years, of conversions to that particular bike that people had done custom work to. Some were done in the Bobber or Cafe Racer Style, but what I was interested in was the scrambler. I thought of it as having a little more rugged outdoor look to it. I did a little research online and there was a company that had custom parts to beef up suspension both front and back. Another company was supplying some moldings to give it that off-road look, Along with a classic Scrambler type retro seat. A company out of Europe had a headlight, signal lights and tail fender conversion also the off-road looking muffler. I started ordering the parts and within a few weeks they were at the shop. I took out the chalkboard and started with the list of what had to be done, itemized priorities along with what needed to be bagged/tagged and what photos needed to be taken. The guys were happy to work on something other than commercial trucks for the next month. Change is sometimes as good as a vacation, particularly when you're being paid for it.

Shop jobs like this are usually lighter work. Also, the clock wasn't being watched and you could do the best job you could, Depending on your equipment and your experience. You could take a little more pride in your work by slowing things down. Thinking things through. No one to blame but yourself if things go for shit.

The engine was in pretty good shape, we just had to replace a few seals on the drive line. Two high-quality spark plugs were put in. The valves were adjusted. Carbs well, I would get them synchronized at the motorcycle shop. The coils were changed in the front shocks along with the rear shocks as a complete unit. The brakes were pulled apart both front and back pads replaced, and calipers inspected. Flushing out the brake fluid then reassembled. The electrical work was straightforward. Just splicing in the new wiring for the new lights and signals. Parts were set aside to be taken to the paint shop. The rims had been taken off and spray-painted semi-gloss black. 80/20 off road tires were put on that gave it a nice aggressive off-road look. I have decided on a Phoenician blue. Probably due to the story I had read recently about the indigenous Mayans and the vision two children had had when they were searching for water up in the mountains. The story goes that the children had eaten buds off a cactus that turned out to be peyote. They then saw the blue deer that spoke to them, told them to go back to their Village and rains would soon come. Kind of like when I read the article about the crack head who killed his wife and kids a few years ago and was soon getting out, back into society. Was the blue deer trying to tell me something? Well time for him later. I also thought motorcycles looked a bit like deer's tromping down the road. The bike was assembled finally the seat and off-road handlebars were put on. The finished product looks pretty good, clean lines the classic retro scrambler look. For the next few weeks when any of the guys in the shop or myself had a free moment we would ride it around the building, trying to practice are wheelies.

The Shop had started to get busy as usual in the spring. The bike was tarped up and rolled off into the corner, waiting for the rains to clear up, probably only 3 or 4 months. And that was usually May in British Columbia. I had other things on my mind for the next few months.

This year the world masters was in Tokyo. It was expected to be the biggest World Masters Judo tournament organized to date. I had registered for it a few weeks earlier and had been training hard for years with little or few injuries. I had been competing in 3 to 10 tournaments a year for the last 6 years. But this was the biggest one for my age and weight group. I had started to double up my training which was normal before a bigger tournament. Usually backing off the week before giving my body time to recover. Judo workouts four to six times a week, heavy weights twice. I was having no problem handling guys half my age at local tournaments at least at a provincial level. The guys in Tokyo would be my age. 40 to 45 years old's, but they were ringers. X national champions some had been Olympians. Or just hadn't stopped training since they were kids, they still love the sport and love to fight. It wasn't going to be any cakewalk. At some of the smaller World Judo Master tournaments, as many as 50% were just recreational with very little tournament experience. These are people who train 2 days a week and very seldom if ever competed. There's a big difference between a club fighter and a tournament fighter. It's pretty easy to go through those guys, to get the finals that's where the ringers are. The bigger tournaments like the Canadian Nationals or the US Nationals it drops down to about 30% of the fighters are recreational. Tokyo is not going to be like that. No one travels across the world to compete in a tournament if they're not competitive. Out of the 46 registered competitors there's probably only going to be two or three recreational guys, they would get taken out early. The rest were ringers and they're representing the country they came from. I had enough air miles on my Visa to get myself around trip in first class.

The Sensei of the club that I had been training out of for the last 10 years, set up a hotel near the venue. The Tokyo Dome Hotel, walking distance to the Kodokan, which is the mecca of Judo. I was booked in there for four nights. Good security, lots of people keeping an eye on things. After the fourth night, I was to stay three nights at my coach's coach home. then back to Canada. The turnout was great, about 1,400 competitors had registered. The organizers had been running tournaments out of there for 50 years, both they and the referees were as good as it gets.

The first couple of fights I got through without too much trouble. The French guy I was fighting in the second or third fight must have gotten a little tunnel vision. He was down by quarter point. He didn't realize it, but your called on stalling pretty quickly at this level. With only a minute and a half left I just kept him at bay and didn't take any chances. A couple of light attacks nothing that could be countered. Two more penalties were called on each of us. I knew it was going on and so did the ref. The fight was over, I'd won the match by quarter point and had not taken any chances. I Shrugged and nodded to the ref, he knew what was going on and so did I. The 4th fight was the toughest one. The guy was a grinder with good balance, strong and obviously had a lifetime of Judo behind him. He was ahead by a quarter point with 30 seconds left. The last trick up my sleeve Is to let them think that I've given up. A sigh and a slight slumping of the shoulders, then wait for his attack. When you're fighting against the Japanese, it's hard for them not to want that big ippon. Crowds love it, they love it, you look like a hero. And that's what he was going to try, he came in hard attempting a big shoulder technique as I expected. But instead of pushing him away what is what most people do, I pulled him towards me. Then sidestepped, this put him off balance for an eighth of a second. This gave me time to drop down, slide my left hand between his legs, keeping my right hand on his lapel. I moved in with my chest against his body, it took a few steps to get his feet off the ground. His toes are now stepping along the ground, with a little more lift they were off the ground. Rotating him in midair with my right hand, he landed flat on his back with me on top of him. He was in shock, shaking his head back and forth and no doubt wondering what the hell happened. I got up and looked at the referee, he smiled, I could see he was chuckling him to himself. Probably wondering how his countrymen have been sucked in by this old Canadian. It was all good fun and I had pulled a rabbit out of my ass and made it to the finals to fight for first place.

I had not been fighting at my best throughout that day. I felt strong with no injuries, but I was a bit heavy on my feet. The humidity had been in the 70 percent range for the last three days. I now had four hours to hydrate, relax and clear my head. I was given 30 minutes notice before the fight. I did the light warm up with one of the guys on the side of the mat. My name is called, and I headed up to the mat area. I was fighting a Japanese guy, who looked calm, relaxed and at least 10 years younger than me. We bowed and both stepped forward. We both took relaxed grips. He stepped forward, I did a bit of a sidestep and moved into a throw I had practiced thousands of times over 15 years on a bungee cord attached to a tree in the backyard. I caught his left foot with my right foot well it was in mid-air. Pulling with my right arm and lifting his elbow with my left he was now in midair. The throw is called sassa-taseracome-asse and my timing had been perfect. I was able to turn his body in midair, he landed on his back with be on top of him. The fight was over in under 5 Seconds. My opponent shook It off and the referee gave me the eyebrow in the air and a small nod. I had won first place at one of the toughest Master tournaments in the world In Tokyo Japan at the Kodokan. I talked to my opponent after the fight, his English was pretty good. He asked what throw I had used and if I would demonstrate it. I told him I had been training on a bungee cord tied to a tree for 15 years and that I thought it helped with the timing. He nodded and smiled, probably chalked it up to a bit of experience. We both had a pretty good story to tell about that day. It was a good day.

I met up with my coach's sensei and a good friend of his later that day. They asked how the fights went. I told them I'd won first place, but they shouldn't worry because, second third and fourth all went to the Japanese. They thought that was funny and also that we needed beer to celebrate. We headed back to their neighborhood and knocked back a lot of beer. A day later I was back on the plane heading home.

What happens after a tournament is you need some down time. You've been on creatine and protein powder most of the season. Its needed to maintain your weight and recovery times. If you continue using it in the off season when you're not training 5 to 7 times a week you would put on too much weight. The draw back is when you cut off it and go back to a normal diet, you tend to feel tired, run down. It lowers your energy level. And as expected you start to feel burnt out. When you physically peak at something, you just can't maintain that forever it's common in older athletes to look a little tired, run down. its not your imagination, your bone tired.

Just borderline being burnt-out. You can still do your daily job, but you know your not at a 100 percent. When you push yourself to the maximum of your ability and then try to maintain that for a years on end. There are peaks and valleys. And they swing as much in both directions. When you need a break, you tend to pull back and try to eat healthy and enjoy the moment. Within a few weeks your back to who you were. It's not unusual to replay events in your mind over and over. Revaluating those split decisions and considering alternative outcomes and scenarios whether you've won or lost.

What I did was dug back into my day job, Running the office and doing the overflow in the shop. Then I started thinking about a road trip on the motorcycle, it would get me off by myself and clear my head. Oh, ya and the unfinished business. As in a debt that needed to be collected.

A good friend had passed away, He lived up in the interior of British Columbia. He was a friend I had known for years, hung around with as teens, we had picked up girls, raced cars and got in the odd bar altercation. Ya we would joke about our screw ups later in life. But we kept in touch, vacationed with our wives together. Some good memories. 30 years later we would still phone each other on a Friday or Saturday night after we had had a few drinks and shoot the shit for an hour. I was a groomsman in his wedding party. He always asked about my boys as they were growing up. And I about his wife, parents and brother. Lots of water under the bridge. We would get together two or three times a year, always talk about the old days and the new days. His wife and family had decided to postpone the funeral services for two months. Most of us that new him were to upset to talk or deal with for the first month. He was 56 and had planned to retire in the fall. 30 years with the city and had a good pension. A life well planned. I decided to fit the motorcycle trip in with funeral along with a few visits to old friends.

CHAPTER 2

I had lots of time to organize the bike trip. I contacted an off-road group and asked if anyone had taken the route, I had planned this year. Someone had, the road was basic but doable on a motorcycle. The bike was a little over 300 lb. You could only do 10 or 20 km an hour, so I planned on two days. I would need an extra gallon and a half of fuel to pack along. Tracing the service road on Google maps wasn't too hard. But it's not always the same when you get out there on the road. Maps or images could be a few years old. The road starts in Harrison Hot Springs. It's called Harrison West Road but after five km, there're no more signs. After 300 km, the forestry service road ends up connecting to the number 1 Hwy. There might be a few small farms but not much else. I thought a couple of days would do that section. I had extra fuel and camping gear to spend the night. Oh, and a nice compact sawed-off shotgun. Sometimes yelling at a bear or people coming to your camp at night just doesn't work. After that it's on to Boston Bar, Hells Gate and up into the Lower Nicola Valley, then Merritt. Weather was expected to be dry, no concern with wash outs.

It's still an active logging road so when ya hear the big trucks you pull over, not just think about it. A loaded logging truck coming down even a slight grade takes time to stop, when traveling at 40 or 50 km even longer. But even on a one lane road there usually room to squeeze a motorcycle against the bank or ditch. Well I gave myself 3 days to get to the funeral, I double checked my bags and loaded up the bike. I usually sleep in my clothes with a thick canvas bag for cover. I gassed up and geared up then I headed out of town through the back roads of Mission. I stopped for coffee at The Wigwam Inn after about an hour on the road. Then headed over to Harrison taking the West road into the mountains. There are always a few campers up in the back-logging roads, in a pinch I can always buy another gallon of fuel. I had a topographic map of the area along with a download of the route in my GPS.

Last two weeks had been busy, few extra shifts and longer hours to get caught up for the week I was going to take off. My wife had decided to drive up with an old friend, I would meet at midday at the hotel. It was nice to get off the paved road. Within half an hour all sign of human humanity disappeared, just me and a back road feeling the gravel against my tires under the bike. Within another hour I made it to the far end of the lake about a hundred kilometers. I pulled over in a small clearing to stretch my legs and pour myself a cup of tea. On the map that showed a small Indian village probably just a few houses. I wouldn't expect there to be many jobs out in the middle of nowhere. Maybe just some service road work or checking the odd camp-site, restocking wood perhaps. A pickup truck pulled in and a couple guys got out. I gave him a nod even though they seem to be annoyed at something. Neither of them looked like they had ever worked a day in their lives. Kind of that soft doughy looking face and bodies with small fingers and hands. It was around noon and they looked like they had just got-ten out of bed. These two had decided they didn't like me. Apparently, I was on some sort of ancestral land. I had checked the maps before I left, and I wasn't. There was some discussion, they seem to think that this was all their land. It was just a matter of time in the Courts. I nodded then said, "you shouldn't count on it". I told them to fuck off or there was going to be trouble, while sipping my tea. They made a few threatening remarks along with gestures, and of course they're going to come back with help. I knew there weren't too many people out here even on a busy day, I wasn't too worried and haven't finished my tea yet. I finished my sand-wich along with tying my gear back up. Well, the pickup truck pulled back in but now they had four people. Apparently two-on-one wasn't enough to threaten someone. The two pudgy guys along with a leaner looking guy in his late twenties get out. Still no concern with the pudgy guys, But the lean fit guy looks like he might work for a living most likely, but probably overconfident due to living in such a small pond. He was also ugly, he looked like he might have been dropped on his head a few times as a kid. Fourth guy a little less native probably only a quarter or a half. He looked a bit on the bright side, not threatening or posturing. Kinda like he had just been dragged into something he didn't want anything to do with. He looked out a place actually, he obviously knew these people, but there have been some time and distance between them. Two pudgy guys started yammering on that I had no right to be here and that I've been rude to them. Again, I told him to fuck off. Well they didn't like that and one of them started coming at me kind of aggressively. I still had my Kevlar jacket on with elbow and shoulder pads. My jeans were Kevlar lined with built in knee protectors. On my feet were a solid pair of motorcycle boots with a heavy shank and ankle protectors. I'd slipped my riding gloves back on well they were getting out of the truck. Also, Kevlar with a nice set of knuckle protectors. You'd have to be an idiot to pick a fight with someone geared up like this. Particularly if they're relaxed, alert and not backing down. I'm pretty sure with those boots I could kick through plywood maybe not half inch but at least ⅜. These guys were obviously as dumb as they looked. The ding dongs were in summer clothes, skinny guy, had a set of work boots on. The others, all runners, light jeans and t-shirts. This wasn't going to go good for them. The first chubby guy comes at me with his hand out a little too far ahead of his two other friends. He looked a little heavy on his feet and I doubted whether he could change directions even if he wanted. It's always better to get the first punch in. There's a certain shock value to it. He was gesturing at me with his leading hand and fingers which gave me a half a second to assess his timing. I paired his hand stepping forward at the same time then hit him as hard as I could at the point of the nose. I could hear and feel cartridge snap on my knuckles. It wasn't a knockout punch, but he dropped to his knees. Blood was coming out of both nostrils like a slow running tap. I then side-stepped to the right and kicked the second chubby guy in the inside of his shin. If the angle is right, you can sometimes chip the person's bone there. The pain is immediate and runs to the skull as if someone has stuck a nail between your eyes. His hands drop down, I reached behind his head and pull it towards me as easily as a pumpkin on a string, at the same time pushed off my back leg and punching him in the jaw where it connects to the skull. Nothing like 25 lb head and a 25 lb fist and arm coming together fast. He dropped like a rock and would probably need his jaw wired shut or three or four weeks.

The lean guy, I thought might give me the most trouble was circling around fast. My breathing was still easy and relaxed, my core was tightening up a bit, the adrenaline had started to kick in. My legs and hands both felt light and fast, no heavy feet here. He was moving faster than the first two and probably could take a few punches. Fourth guy still standing there watching all. He seemed to have a little smile on his face, but no threat yet. That could be good or bad and in another ten seconds I would probably find out.

One guy on his knees with blood pouring out of his nose, like a slow running faucet, was pretty funny to see if it's not your own. Then the next guy was up close and throwing punches they were fast; trades workers have that skill set. But you can see them coming, his shoulder would drop down, arm would cock back 5 or 10 inches. Then his whole body and shoulder would swing at you. There was at least a second to second and a half to react, no problem after 25 years of martial arts training. I had had enough playing around. I grab him around the back of the head and pulled it down, at the same time my right knee came up hard into his lower floating ribs. Twice just to make sure. I could feel my knee sink in four to six inches. Just like I practiced on a heavy bag for years. Both arms dropped to his sides then to his chest. I could hear him gasping in short breaths. I stretched out one of his arms by the wrist with very little resistance. With one hand I folded it back onto itself. A basic one hand wrist lock. With my free hand I gave the back of his knuckles quick palm punch. Definitely bones crunching this time. He wasn't going to move or cause me trouble. When bones are broken a wave of pain and nausea rushes through the body. Most people just sit down or back away to try to protect themselves from further injury, and that's exactly what he did.

The guy with the bleeding nose had gotten up and decided to do some sort of bear tackle. The type where they kinda hunch over and start charging you. It looks like they're trying to ram you in the stomach with their head. I sidestep to the left matching his speed and was able to drive is head and face into the ground. I gave him three sharp short kicks in the side of the ribs. He rolled on his side and stopped moving.

I started moving towards the young guy by the truck. Assessing him, there was no threat. I slowed down my breathing, in through the nose out through the mouth as if I was trying to blow out a candle. I spent a few extra seconds processing what has happened. I walked up to him slowly with my palms facing up. I meant him no harm. He nodded; he said his name was Jake. I then asked what the story was? Why were these guys coming after me? Well they were the local bullies in the tribe in a very small community. These three guys have picked on him as a kid, he wasn't too upset to see them get some payback. He had been at University for the last two years, and had just come back for the summer, to help with administration, possibly to set up some developmental programs. In the two years that he had been away, these three jackasses had taken to harassing campers or people traveling along the road. They had the delusion that somehow, they were owed something even though they had worked very little in their lives. They had lost all self-respect, and now thought if they had enough money, they could just buy it back. Jake packed them up into the pickup truck. He was going to drive them down for a check over at the doctor's office. It gave him time to think about the final draft of a prosed developmental plan he was finishing off at the end of this season. The tribal council were looking for some sort of ten step plan, he knew it would never work. It would just be another lie to tell themselves rather than just getting a job.

He thought he was going to catch some shit for not helping in the fight. I said that's true but at least they have someone to drive them to the hospital. I watched him drive away then got back on my bike headed east. The tension had drifted away from me as it always does. Within 20 minutes I was one with the bike heading up a road by a riverbed into the mountains.

The service roads in that area are usually well maintained. Compacted crushed gravel with a ditch on the hill side if its needed. Wooden or concrete bridges over the creeks. Within half an hour I couldn't see any fresh tracks in front of me. The pace was still 20 to 40 kl an hour, it was windy. There's a lot of shale mixed in with the gravel, which is fine when it is dry, but with a little water on it, it gets greasy. You just must slow down around any corners. Then you can drive it all day long without a problem. And that's what I was going to do. I put on about 50 km on before I pulled over for a stretch. I had gone through a few valleys, some of them had been logged in the last few years, other sections looked like 30 or 40 years of growth.

It always surprises me how quiet it is when you shut the engine off in the middle of nowhere. I was probably at least 50 km from any other humans. The only sound I could hear was the rustling of leaves from the wind blowing through the trees. There was also the slight sound of water running somewhere in the distance diffused by the trees. Time to get back on the bike. I started up and headed on my way again. I wasn't in any rush. I had planned to put another hour in riding, then look for a place to camp. Usually in the backcountry you'll find a pull outs by most streams, lakes or ponds. Usually used by campers in the summer, hunters in the fall, they're the same types of places people have stopped for the night, for thousands of years when traveling.

I came by a pickup truck with two guys in it and their gear in the back. We slowed as we approached each other on the road. Eyed each other up, then stopped and talked. They come up to the backwoods to do some foraging and a bit of target shooting. They also check out the game trails for the fall hunting season. They asked where I was headed. I told them through to the old number 1 Highway, but that I would spend the night somewhere along the road. They said that they had done the same run a month and a half earlier and didn't think I would have any problems. I asked them if there were any good camping spots up ahead. They said," yup a couple on the right and one on the left, all had pull outs". They hadn't seen anyone else in two days, it should be pretty quiet. The water was good this year, no beaver fever. They also haven't seen any active logging. No chance of getting run over by a logging truck. If you're the only one there, expect to have it yourself for the night. I told him that's what I was looking for a quiet night. They nodded and said they knew what I meant. We headed on our ways.

Within 15 minutes I came to the first pull out. It looked a little too low and damp, I was looking for something a little more open, the trees sparse to get some light through. I turned around and headed back on the road for another ten minutes. The second spot had been cleared and had a fire pit with some leftover wood around it. The stream was close by and it connected to a small lake. I set up my tarp and hammock. It should keep me off the ground and dry even if it rained. It wasn't long before I had a fire going. Smoke and crackling usually keeps the animals away. I made a tripod out of a few branches and hung my tin pot with my stew in it to warm up. I did a walk around the camp, there was a trail beside the creek that led down to the lake. Other than that, just a few small game trails.

I found an old outhouse, which was just a four-inch log strung between two low lying branches, with a small dugout area in the ground. Looked like the previous campers or hunters had been good enough to all use the same spot. No one wants to step in shit in the middle of the forest. I still had some tea left in the thermos. I might as well find a soft spot to sit with my back against a tree and run through it again, in my mind how I'm going to kill that mother fucker.

The stew turned out pretty good, didn't take long to warm up. I finished it up along with some slices homemade bread I had brought with me. I was feeling pretty warm both in body and mind. Still had an hour of daylight so I took out my bush knife and practice my throwing on a half rotten stump ten feet away. It took five minutes, but I got my timing back. After that I was getting four-inch groupings, throwing the knife as hard as I could. I can't think of any good reason to throw a good tool such as a knife. But like darts or archery it helps focus your attention. It seems to awaken something in me.

I hung a LED light from the tarp, laid out my sleeping bag. I set the sawed off 12 gauge with the mag light strapped to the barrel in the hammock. It had been cut off at both the barrel and the stock. Then I added a sling with pockets for eight rounds. Four buck shot, four slugs one in the chamber. It was only a single barrel with a heavy hammer and pull, but I could shoot and reload in three seconds. Not a world record but I could do it with my eyes closed. No chance of it going off on its own either. Unlike the bullshit stories in every safety manual of the hunter going off and shooting himself in the head by accident. There aren't many places where a bear or cougar is going to bother you in British Columbia, but it does happen every year. The more concerning predators are human. If someone comes into your campsite after dark, it's just asking for trouble. And I'm not talking a public or provincial parks camp-sites. Out in the bush as in no man's land. There aren't any witnesses out in the middle of nowhere. You best keep your bullshit to the city.

It was getting dark and I'd had a good piss. Time to hit the sack. I climbed in the hammock without tipping it over and into the sleeping bag. There were a few logs on the fire that should smol-der throughout the night to keep the animals away. There was that deep quiet you can't get in the city. No hum from neon lights or refrigerators. No creak-ing from air conditioning or heating systems warm-ing and cooling. Just the sound of a few crickets and a light breeze blowing through the trees with the slow running creek nearby. I woke up around 11:30 pm. I could hear rustling in the bushes nearby. A few minutes later clicking sounds. Now I know these are usually just from raccoons, but it's a little annoy-ing. It sounds like something out of an alien movie. Along with that I could hear the rustling of mice or muskrats scurrying around the campsite. There seems to be a party going on and I wasn't invited. After listening closely for at least five minutes I got out of the hammock with the shotgun, turned on the mag light and checked my camping spot, also the surrounding bushes. It was quiet when I walked around. No eyes peeking from behind the shrubs or trees. I got back in the sleeping bag and forced myself back to sleep. I dreamed the same dream, like I had many times before.

An older house on a bluff near the water. The ground begins to shake and the earth cracks and opens. The land along the shore begins to separate from the mainland. The waters are always deep and turbulent. The house is always just on the edge, but never falls in. I'm just an observer nothing more. Sometimes when the shore separates from the mainland the waters begin to calm. I'm now standing on an island a mile from the shore with cliffs on all sides and the house is still attached to the Island close to the edge. I force the waters to calm and the sun to come back out. The dream ends. Sleeping out in the forest by yourself may seem like an adventure. Some might think it's risky, but your only real danger are humans and there weren't any of those around. The noise of the forest at night woke me up several more times. I was pretty sure every critter for quarter mile had come to see what the human was up to. At five a.m. it all got quiet again. I slept till 6:15 am then got my ass out of bed. It was a clear day and the ground was still wet with dew. The fire had gone out. With a little kindling and the rest of the wood lying around the campsite it was back up and burning in ten minutes. I washed up and continued with my morning business. Fresh water was hanging from the coffee pot waiting to come to a boil. I tossed some onions, peppers and bacon into the old frying pan. I thought I'd let those cook for a while before draining the grease and adding the eggs. Half an hour later, I was washing my face and packing up my gear. My plan was to drive another 50 kilometers before stopping for a break.

I was getting in my groove, powering up the hills then letting the engine compression take me down, very seldom touching the brakes. I was at the top of one of these hills when a Bobcat crossed the road in front of me. He stopped up on the opposite bank and stared at me for a while. I'd slowed down and stopped by then. Its always amazes me what perfect coats cats, wild foxes and wolves have in the wild. They seem to always have that relaxed alert look in their eyes. Like a fighter at the top of this craft on game day. That Bobcat had no fear or concern of me. Just observed then went on his way. A fighter at the top of his game.

CHAPTER 3

Brian Cannon was enjoying being out of prison. Even though the halfway house would be his home for the next year. The anger management courses were still mandatory. He wasn't the one that caused his anger, it was always other people. But oh no he couldn't say that, always had to tell them what they wanted to hear. He had learned a few things in prison over the last seven years. He still had a lump on his head from getting the crap beat out of him twice in the first two weeks of his sentence while in general population. They, the other inmates don't like child killers. He had tried to explain it was his wife's fault that didn't help. Word was spreading through the prison that he was going to be killed if he wasn't moved. Even convicted felons have some jailhouse code. Well most of them anyway, he was transferred into the pedophile psych wing of the Edmonton Maximum Security Prison for his own protection. He was disgusted having to be associated with these perverts. But he would try to manage. Maybe there was a few courses he could take to pass the time. Over the years he had gotten to know a few of the other inmates, they weren't that bad. It was a disease; they couldn't help themselves just like him. One of the inmates Billy Ray, whom he talked to daily had talked about grooming kids slowly. Letting them know how much you love and cared for them. With time you could usually do whatever you wanted to them. Explaining that your love was unconditional. Billy Ray was serving time in jail for molesting three boys over a two-year period, in a daycare. What they didn't know was there were dozens more that he had gotten away with. It's probably why he always had a smug look on his face. Sometimes people would ask about it. He would just smile, nod and tell them he just liked to look at the sunny side of life.

What Billy Ray didn't know was that he was also on the same list as Brian and the people keeping track of the list also knew of the dozens of other children he had molested and gotten away with. When he was finished serving his easy time and back out on the streets it wouldn't be long before he found himself at the bottom of the Fraser River weighted down with chain. It's too bad the dog food plant was shut down after being condemned. It had been supplying a great public service for thirty years. It was a nice easy way to get rid of bodies. Then the whole DNA science came into use, putting an end to easy cheap disposal. Everybody covering their asses.

Brian didn't think of himself as a danger to

society and he had done his time. He was reformed. On his release, Correctional services had set him up a job, at a tire retread plant. It was dirty and physical, but the pay was okay. On the upside he had already found a supplier of hillbilly heroin or "oxy" for short. It turned off those dreams he had to put up with while he was in prison. Just crush up the Oxycontin tabs, add some water to it in a spoon and a little heat to dissolve it. Then shoot it up. Thank God for those four pillars of harm reduction and the free needle exchange program. No questions asked, you got to love Canada. He needed to get his ass to work tomorrow it was Friday. There would be nothing going in his arm tonight. Fridays were always a little slack at work. Half the crew would be hungover and that would slow down everyone else. Just the way he liked it.

He fell asleep early and dreamed the dream he would rather not. There he was again on the old stained couch in his trailer. The smell of rancid sweat was all around him. Thick red blood covered his hands and sleeves. There was an old ball-peen hammer beside him on the couch. He felt tired, like he was coming off a good high. But his arms and chest were heavy. Memories came back to him. His wife was going to leave him the next day and take the kids with her. The argument had been loud and vicious. Susan called him a drug addict. He wasn't he was just a casual user and liked to party. She was still yelling at him from the kitchen cleaning up his mess from earlier that day. He would never see his kids again, she said.

The rage was building in him. He felt like he was looking through a tunnel. He decided that if he couldn't have the kids no one could. Especially Josie, the two-year-old, she was Susan's favorite. He quietly got up and went to the closet. The ball-peen hammer was in his right hand now. Brian felt like he was walking through a slow-motion picture. He was now in the kids' room standing above Josie's bed. The rage was still inside of him, As the cold sweat ran off his face. Susie should have never threatened to take the kids away, it's all her fault. The first blow of the hammer landed on Josie the two-year-old, above the left eye. The hammer sunk into the wooden stock. He had to use his left hand against her small head to pull it free. Three more quick hits and the hole was the size of a softball. Brady, the four-year-old had not moved or woken. Brian's heart was racing. Sweat was running down his back through his shirt. Brady was lying face down in the small bed. He hit him in the back of the skull. As he pulled the hammer out, he thought he could hear screaming from somewhere behind him off in the distance. Maybe from outside some-where. It was welfare Wednesday and the neighbors were probably all partying. Susie would never hold Josie or Brady again. Four more quick strikes to the back of his head. Something was now grabbing at him, clawing him like an animal. He turned around quickly, fast and hard. The animal was still clawing at him, Wild out of control. He swung hard into its face again and again. It had dropped to the floor, but he didn't stop. He was blind with rage. The cheek-bone and eye sockets were now caved in. Whatever it was, it was now dead.

Brian walked slowly back to the couch. Re-filled his crack pipe and added a little ground oxy to take the edge off. He felt so heavy in the dream. At least his wife had stopped yelling at him. He was sure there were people standing around the bed talking about him. His body felt stiff or frozen, he couldn't force himself to wake up.

He awoke from his dream in a cold sweat. Brian was looking forward to Friday night. Just a little hillbilly heroin to take the edge off. What harm would it be?

Brian thought about his probation officer before he fell back to sleep. Janice Boden, she had quite the rack on her, even in her forties. There was something about her eyes. Like she looked right through him. The fucking bitch needed to be taught a lesson. All his time in prison wasn't a complete waste. He had learnt a little patience. She had it coming.

CHAPTER 4

A couple of hundred yards down the road was that great view. The road was cut into a cliff face. Well, not as good as Number Five Orange in downtown Vancouver in the late seventies, but it was pretty good. There's something about being able to see things coming. Wouldn't that be nice. Brakes were squeaking a bit, probably just dust or silt on the pads. Quick check before I headed down the hill showed no abnormality. Hydraulic level looked okay, ready to go. My estimates were that by noon I would be going through the small forestry town of Boston Bar. 12:15 pm, humm a pretty good estimate. I stopped at Smitty's restaurant in town for a light lunch, soup and sandwich, barley vegetable soup with a tuna sandwich. Mostly locals and truckers with a few retired guys thrown in. The waitress was pleasant but had that look in her eyes, like she had lost trust in humanity. There was probably a story there, but my plate was full, and I had a schedule to keep.

This section of Number 1 Highway from Boston Bar to Lower Nicola Road is a great run on a dry day. It's a mountainous region of BC with the

Fraser River running through it. The highway passes through Hell's Gate the narrowest section on the Fraser River. Mountains on one side and the mighty Fraser on the other. It's estimated that a million dollars of gold dust is taken down that River a year and never claimed. Only to be washed out to the Sea or laid in the riverbed's long slower-moving sections. The traffic was light which gave me time to plan. Brian Cannon would be dead in three days, weighted down in the slough beside the Fraser River.

My old friend, Janice, in Kamloops had been keeping track of him getting out of prison. Where he lived, his new job, and his shopping routines. His curfew was 10 p.m. to 6 a.m. He wasn't going to be doing anything that she didn't know about. She even helped him get set up with his drugs, without any trace getting back to her. She was calm and always methodical. That skill set had always helped her in her line of work. Leave the emotion out of it, save that for a good roll in the hay.

Nicola Road is quiet and winding with very little traffic. It runs alongside the Nicola River, by old school ranches, hobby farms and one small Indian reserve. Great riding in the summer. I got into the city of Merritt around 2:30 p.m. Then back to my wife and friends at the hotel. The service for my good friend Brent was to start at 4:30 p.m. then a buffet at 6 p.m. I was a little stiff from the ride but clear-headed. I hadn't seen some of the old friends in years. Some I hardly recognized. We all headed off to the service, it was held in his father's ranch house. Brent was too young to die. He had led an honorable life and had many new and lifelong friends to attest to that. He would be missed by many but not forgotten. His wife of 30 years had not adjusted yet to the loss, but she had close family and friends to help her through this time.

It wasn't so much funeral but a celebration of life. Both old and young friends along with this fellow engineering associates said their peace. He would be missed by all. The ride back to the hotel was uneventful. My wife and her friends headed back by car and me, well, I had a little more of the motorcycle trip that I wanted to do. I stayed at a hotel suggested, due to the proximity to an underground parking lot full of cars that I could borrow for the night. The benefit of being a truck shop owner is that you can buy sets of keys to unlock a variety of vehicles; domestics or imports 5 to 15 years old. They are only available to dealers, shop owners and are referred to as master keys sets. I checked into the hotel in Kamloops. Then changed into my gray man clothes. These, I had picked up and used to help me look like a local tradesman or city worker. All very nondescript including pair of glasses and baseball hat. I went to the underground parking lot and started my vehicle search. I was looking for a 10 to 15-year-old domestic or import, that appeared in good shape but a low miler. Usually these are used by people who don't drive much. Perhaps once or twice a week and dealer serviced, with practice they're not hard to spot. Probably owned by a retired person. Preferably gray or brown something that would blend in, mid-sized, nondescript. There it was, a 95 gray Toyota Camry. Third key in the set opened the door, the second key worked the ignition. Interior was clean, the backseat looked like it had never been used. I thought I got a faint whiff of Pine-Sol. Definitely an old man car. I headed over to the alley, parked in a dimly lit area, but I knew Brian would walk by in 30 or 40 minutes.

I got the text by someone who was watching the bar that Brian had just left. No one else had been in or out of the alley in 30 minutes. I took the plastic bottle rum and drained a small amount out of it. Then sat down and leaned against the wall in the alley. I set the bottle down beside me with the lid back on. There's no way he would pass up a free bottle that wasn't traced to him. Brian walked into the alley and saw me lying there. He walked up and stopped by my feet.

Jesus Christ, Brian said to himself, "I can't believe my luck, a friendly drunk guy and a full bottle of booze. Why couldn't everyone be like this, nice to me, that's all I've ever wanted".

In my best slurred voice, I asked him if he wanted to pull. That's slang for drink. As he reached down, I grabbed him by the collar and pulled him in and down. Wrapping my legs around his waist at the same time. I wrapped one arm then behind his neck palm to palm. Right shoulder under his chin, putting pressure upward. He tried to lift up, as expected.

What the fuck, Brian said to the drunk, "mother fucker, I'm going to..." But his throat was now cut off. What the fuck, he thought as the pain increased. A black cloud and pain were the last things he remembered as he began to lose consciousness.

I release one leg and kicked his knee out. Collapsing him on top of me. His back was now arched with his windpipe blocked. With my feet I pushed his hips down further. The pressure on his neck and throat were now unbearable. Brian passed out from the pain. I could feel him go limp. Rolling him over I quickly broke his neck. All was still quiet in the alley. I dragged him by the collar over to the car trunk. One hand on him and one on the bottle of rum. He was loaded in the trunk with ease. The tarp I had laid in the trunk wouldn't leave any trace of him. A quick look around, always double check for anything's that had been left behind or had fallen out of a pocket. It was as clean as a whistle. Time to deliver him to his resting spot.

Twenty minutes later I was on a deserted gated road that ran along the dike by a slough.

Those master keys certainly have come in handy over the years. I found the landing along the dyke and beside the slough that I was looking for. The two cinder blocks, chain and rope were right where they were supposed to be. Brian was soon chained up and weighted down and the rope was run through the tie straps between his wrists. The two loose ends of the rope were weighed and then tossed to the other bank of the slough. Ten minutes later I was on the other side of the slough with the two ends of the rope dragging Brian into the middle where the mud is soft and deep. I released one end of the rope then pulled the entire length of rope in with the other. The mud was soft in this area, within a few hours he would be three feet deep stuck in it. In a week maybe five feet down. Just like the good old days in the English moors. The walk back to the car gave me time to clear my head. It was a clear night I could feel the dew in the air. Not sure why but it seemed to bring some closure for me. I wasn't sure it was for my old friend, or for the murdered mother and her two children.

The gate to the dike was closed and locked. None the wiser. The rope was tossed in a ditch a few miles down the road. The tarp was chucked in the garbage bin of the underground parking. The car checked over, wiped down and seat readjusted. It seemed like a long day, I was hungry and needed a good night's sleep.

CHAPTER 5

Best to get out of the gray man clothes and into my street duds. I slipped off shoes, jacket and pants outside my room and bagged them. The rest when I was in the room. A quick shower, dressed, then down to the twenty-four-hour cafe at the end of the block. Coffee and an omelette hit the spot. It was one of those old-time coffee shops you still see in downtowns, remnants from the post war boom of the '50s when people still met for coffee in the morning to find out what's happening around town. Brown upholstery, off white walls, checkered tile floor and a 24-hour breakfast menu. I had picked a booth rather than a seat at the counter. No sense in exposing my back, even if I'm not expecting problems.

Janice had access to the only two cameras that had recorded me coming and going from the alley or the Hotel. She had deleted both for a seven-day period. They would start a new loop in the morning. She had also seen me enter the restaurant and thought a coffee with an old friend would be a nice end to the evening.

I saw her walk in. I had forgotten how good looking she was, Shoulder length brown wavy hair. Clear calm blue eyes and very shapely curves in all the right places. She smiled and asked if she could join me.

She had known Max Jobber since high school. He seemed to be getting better looking with age. Not the vee waist he used to have but a relaxed confidence that had grown with age. They had had a fling between high school and university, and it was great. She still wondered from time to time "what if'. She remembered back on the time in her first year of university when an English professor had started dropping her grades, then suggested to her, that regular sex with him would improve them again. By chance she had bumped into Max the same week and told him the story. Max had listened quietly, waiting for her to finish. Then said, "you have friends Janice, you're not alone, if you want his legs broken just let me know". She never took Max up on the offer, but it gave her the confidence to solve the problem professor's libido with a few words. Janice wondered what Max saw when he looked at her. It always felt like he was reading her mind, looking into her soul. She asked him if he remembered those summer nights when they were dating. He said he did with a smile and then asked if she was going to come back to the hotel with him. Her heart started beating faster but she managed to say, yes.

Max wasn't sure what had gotten into him, but it felt like they were eighteen again. Sneaking back to his parents' house for a good lay. Just holding her hand and walking down the street brought back those old memories of the summer nights. He could feel the same lump in his pants that was always there whenever he touched her.

Janice knew he would make love to her as he had years earlier. Like a hungry animal that had been let off a leash. A combination of lust and passion that she had never found elsewhere. She still loved her husband and he loved her but like a lot of middle-aged people they had fallen into a rut, sexually. She knew when things slowed down and they had more time for each other that it could be rekindled. She slipped out of Max's arms, dressed then headed home. Max, well just like when he was eighteen, had fallen asleep after making love and was now snoring. It always surprised her how Max could turn it on and off with a flip of a switch. Passion or violence was always under his control.

I woke up to the scent of Janice on the sheets and my mind. Jasmine and peaches, I'm not sure how she did that. I spent the next 45 minutes going through my core exercises and yoga while processing logistics and the movements of the night before. I searched for flaws, inefficiencies or careless mistakes. A ten-minute hot shower loosened me up and cleared my head. Another two minutes of straight cold water while I practised my asana breathing techniques, to finish it off. It was a clear dry day and I was looking forward to getting the motorcycle back on the road. Three out of the four hours would be highway driving. It will give me a chance to test out the upper speed ranges of the bike. A 1994 K100 BMW should do 200 to 220 kilometers an hour. But this one had a few modifications to the suspension and tires along with the fairings removed also some dual sport off road tires. 190 kilometers an hour is what I'm looking for at the top end.

The commuter traffic had cleared, not that there was much to begin with. In ten minutes, I was on the outskirts of town. After twenty minutes, I was on open highway, with no one in front and no one behind, just the way I like it. Just the sound of the engine and the rhythm of the road. I was in the groove; time was slipping away. The story of my past and future laid out in front of me and behind with all the variables like the branches of a tree. Alternative destiny's whether chosen or forced, waiting to be lived or lived at the same time in another reality. All those memories of experiencing that exact same moment it time. They used to call it déjà vu, now, well it just false memories. Even if hundreds or thousands of people have the same memories. It's still all false. The only truths are the ones you are told. You are no longer allowed to have your own or no longer allowed to have your own beliefs. But for now, its was just me and the road. I knew the next section of road for ten kilometers was straight with a few banked curves that could handle higher speeds. I started leaning into the throttle. 140, 160, 180 kilometers an hour. The wind started flapping my jacket and pants. I was crouched down tight against the fuel tank, still watching the road and odometer, now reading 201 kilometers and hour. That was fast enough for me. When I looked up, I was approaching two cars side by side way too fast. A quick decision to split them was the safest option. There was enough room to slow down, the cars looked like they were stopped when I went between them at twice their speed. A few seconds later I checked my mirror, the cars were still side by side cruising down the mostly empty highway. Twenty kilometers later, I backed off the throttle. High speed driving is work, unless you have a death wish. I didn't, I had shit to do and debts to collect. Why leave the shit on the sidewalk when you can wash it of in this life?

I was back down to cruising speed 110 kilometers an hour, not too much buffeting from the wind, but enough to keep me alert. The midway point of this journey was just ahead. Time to gas up and grab a coffee. Traffic was still light; the dew had burnt off and the road ahead was clear with good banked corners. There's about seven kilometers of down hill grade on this stretch before a pull off. In the winter this stretch of road can be a little icy. This time of year, it is no problem at all. I gassed up at my usual spot then walked around to the coffee shop. There were a few people in line, like any where, where you can get a decent cup of coffee. I couldn't help but notice that the guy in front of me had turned slightly and was staring at me. He was large with a doughy body and stuffed into an auxiliary police uniform. I let it go for a few seconds then locked eyes with him, telling him, if he didn't stop staring at me, I would knock his teeth out. I don't mind people challenging me, but not when their hiding behind their job or uniform. It's an act of a bully or coward. There was a full-time constable in front of him, with a couple of stripes on his sleeve, he turned around with a complete poker face to see what was going on. As politely as I could I told him they should stop recruiting at Walmart while nodding my head towards the dim-witted auxiliary guy. The constable with the same dead eyed look, looked towards the ride along, then back towards the counter, shaking his head as he did so. I'm pretty sure he knew what I was talking about and obviously this guy wasn't his first choice as a ride along. Judging by the new recruits' character it would be better to cut him loose as soon as possible. I grabbed my coffee and a seat outside.

While sipping the hot, dark brew I'm not sure why, but I started recalling an event from 20 years earlier. Rerunning it through my head as if it was yesterday. I had heard about Jack Smith through the normal sources. He had molested a few kids' years earlier and had gotten away with it. He wasn't active now, but his name had come up and now the debt was going to be paid. I was to talk to him, give him some options. He was going to admit in writing what he had done and let the chips fall where they may. The talk went as well as could be expected. Jack not saying much. In the end he said he couldn't live with being labeled a sex offender. He talked about hanging himself. That would certainly clear the debt. Most people think of hanging oneself as violent or abrupt. It is not like that, not like that at all. It is quiet and slow, with just a warm feeling engulfing your body. He looped the belt through it's buckle then tied a knot in the other end. The knot was placed over a bedroom door, then the door closed. The looped end was carefully moved around his neck. Slowly relaxing his legs, he applied the pressure. The air is not cut off so it's easy to breathe, no panic, just the blood flow is stopped. The dark cloud of unconsciousness closed around his vision as he passed out. I sat with him for another ten minutes, then checked his pulse. He was done. His family would be spared the news of his arrest. Just a suicide by hanging of a disturbed person, while the classic music of Ode to Joy ran through my head.

I had finished my coffee and was back on an outdoor balcony of a coffee shop in a small town with music still in my mind. The black ground remains of pressed coffee always leave a bitter taste in my mouth, like the dust of a long ride down a dirt road. I headed back on the road into the mountains of the Coquihalla Highway. The view along that stretch, with the snow-covered peaks near the summit is as good as it gets. The air is always fresh clean and cool year-round. There is very little debris on the road in the summer. There're a few spots you can pick up your speed with two lanes in both direction and a divider in the middle. It's not hard to wind it up safely through some of the long cooley's and banked bends around the mountains. Coming down through the Great Bear snow shed is always an adventure. The road darkens up and the lanes converge. If you are lucky, no one has lost their antifreeze or an oil pan. On a motorcycle, well that's a problem. With only a couple of inches of rubber in contact with the road a slick surface oil will drop the bike. Today was all smooth sailing. I wound my way through and into the next valley with 3000 to 5000-foot mountains on either side. It's pretty spectacular even if you are not impressed too easily.

CHAPTER 5

It wasn't hard to get back into the routine at the shop. As usual with most of truck shops there's always customers waiting to get in. Days were filled, jobs completed, and invoices written up. I had been back for about a week when I got the text. As usual it was cryptic, to the average person it wouldn't make sense. Once or twice a year the group met in person with no phones, no cameras, no cell coverage. Just six people randomly meeting on a deserted hiking trail on Crown Land. One of the original members, Sam Sheldon was getting a little long in the tooth. Most of the connections he once had were retired or dead. Sam has been diagnosed with cancer and would be lucky to live another year. At 78 years of age, he thought he had lived a full life. Two wives, five kids, and four grandchildren. He been recruited right out of high school in the early fifties. Mostly on account of his size and his amateur boxing experience. He was a year into his training before they realized he also had a head on his shoulders. He could always easily remember dates, phone numbers and faces, which was quite an asset before computers. Like most police departments in that era they dealt with the shit in their own backyard. You are giving warnings, then a good beating and if that didn't straighten you out and you made the choice to become a full-time criminal, you were removed from society. If you were clever enough to get away with rape, unjustified assaults or murder, but still hadn't been caught yet, well they would send Sam after you. Sam had been raised on a farm and he was quite familiar with the process of culling the herd. There is always a certain percentage of domestic animals or crops that are diseased. Back then, they didn't nurture and cuddle with the hope one who is diseased would come around. It was cut down or they buried it, with no more fuss then trimming one's fingernails. By the 1960's Sam was organizing five or six people to do the same work we did now. Some were just office types or what you would call "watchers", others well they didn't mind getting their hands dirty. Sam was unique, he was both. As he sometimes put it," it was a man's god damn duty to wash the shit off the sidewalks".

Sam had brought in the man who would be his successor, and he had been grooming for several years. Dana Busham was an Iranian, whose family had been killed before the war by local criminals in the old country. Dana spoke five languages which Sam thought would be an asset in this new world. Janice had arrived, calm, with those steady eyes, looking great as usual. Also attending were the others: Shawn, Dave and Chan, who usually worked together as their own team. Chan passed out a new burner phone to each person, along with a USB stick that could be plugged into the charging port of most phones. It was used to send encrypted text to other phones. The software stayed in the USB stick and could not be traced. It also left no record of it sending or receiving on the phone. I was never sure where he got this shit from and hadn't asked. Sam was last to speak; he had been a mentor and friend to all of us. He passed out a second USB stick to all of us with a short description of its contents.

This included a list of contacts both in government and private agencies that owed favors and names of contacts people who donate what's needed to the cause. Also, the latest training manuals and tracking systems info and persons on watch lists. Furthermore, a list of "Sleepers" that could be activated and a few nasty old men and women that don't give a shit or take any shit. Sam once talked about this elderly lady in her seventies that wanted to help out with some park muggings. Elizabeth was a knitter, mostly doilies. He had no idea where she came from, just kept showing up. She liked to sit on a park bench knitting with a purse under her arm, that's all. One particular day, Sam was in the bushes hidden, ten feet away. Sure, as shit, the guy made a grab for the purse. Instead of yelling, the sweet elderly lady, Elizabeth pulls him into her, then punches the ten-inch knitting needle into his throat up into his brain. The mugger dropped on the spot. She then wiped off the knitting needle, put it and the unfinished doilies in her purse, and before she left told Sam that, "dat is how we dealt with criminals when I vus a little girl". Sam, always the pragmatist, also left. He recalled this episode with a rare smile.

Everything had been said that needed to be. The group went their separate ways. Back to their day jobs, so to say.

CHAPTER 6

I was back to the routine of work and running a business. Kids were back in school and a little more time on my hands. The wife, well, not sure what had gotten into her. She had turned into some kind of nymph. I know these things happen from time to time, but it had been two weeks. I was getting a little run down and missing sleep. Three hours of sex a night is difficult to maintain when your still working full time. I guess that happens when you marry a Unicorn. Sometimes I wasn't sure who she was any more. She had some Aussie blood in her, maybe that was where it was coming from. I would wake up in the middle of the night with her jumping up and down on me. Well in a gentle rhythmic way. It wasn't all bad.

I came up with a plan. It wasn't noble, but I thought it would work. I put some shrimp shells in the bottom of the garbage, in a new bag. I had them on brochettes for lunch by myself on the BBQ when no one was home. A day later the garbage was half full, while we were in the kitchen, I mentioned that there was a fishy smell. Sally agreed and smiled and said she would freshen up, with a wink.

Well, the smell lingered in the kitchen over dinner. No one finished their dinner. Me, the kids or Sally, the dishes were cleaned, garbage was taken out. We were back on the couch snuggling and winding down. Then there was the talk. Maybe we could cut back on the two or three-hour sessions a night. Two or three times a week is just fine with me it adds to the romance.

With a cuddle and snuggle, Sally thought that would be just fine. And myself, I had a decent uninterrupted night's sleep.

Except for the dream, the recurring one. I've been having it since my thirties. Another world, another planet almost exactly the same as this one, but not quite. The dream is always lucid, lucid enough that my memories of it are now intertwined with this reality. South America has moved 2000 kilometers. to the east. Cuba now runs East- West instead of North-South. Fiction is presented as fact. Fact is scoffed at as hooky science. All truth has become a gray area. The other earth felt safer, more stable, like less people pulling the strings and more independent thought. Fortunately, the dream only takes up an hour or so, a few nights a year. The bed clothes as usual and myself were drenched in sweat. Not a feverish sweat or cold one, more like a sweat you would want to purify your body and mind. For the first few years that the dream was taking place, I questioned my sanity and reality. On more than one occasion I rechecked old geography atlases that my parents had kept around from the '60s. I had browsed through those books hundreds of times as a child, identifying countries, border longitude latitude lines, South America, North America, Europe, remote Islands and population statistics. They were used as references for geography homework in elementary school. What a surprise it was when I checked 35 years later and the continents, were no longer in the same position that I had seen in the same book years ago. My memories weren't false then and they're not now. I can still remember documentaries in the '70s and '80s, about the formation of the Gulf of Mexico. It was caused by a large meteorite much like the one that created the Hudson Bay in Canada. Years ago, all maps and globes showed a very clear round symmetrical pattern in the Golf of Mexico. With Cuba on the far east side below Florida running north and south. Now, it looks like a piece of cauliflower.

South America is now 1600 nautical miles from Africa. That's all of a 16-day trip in a Viking long boat with a sail. Looks like history is going to have to be changed also, besides the maps if this keeps up. It all started with those damn false memories.

Well, I'm awake anyways, may as well get my ass out of bed before my wife wants some morning sex.

CHAPTER 7

I spent the next few months studying up on the manuals Sam had supplied in the USB stick. One of the information units detailed how loose the entrapment laws are. At one time entrapment was clearly illegal but now, like many things, the gray area about entrapment is wide and deep. Now it is very easy to set up law-abiding people to take a fall, or who needed to be moved out of the way. Also, politicians had now become instruments of highly financed lobbying groups. Most politicians, until they start doing favors, can't afford to pay off their monthly balances on their visas. Within four years of holding office, 90% of them are buying new or upgrading their homes. All of this, on wages less than those of the average trade's person. This section, describing the money flow within the lobbying groups, through layers of organization and companies with agendas that have nothing to do with the interest of the people within that city state or country, was extensive. All of the lobbyists had agendas other than what they were actually saying. Some of the agendas were more to control demographic groups of people, while other agendas wanted exclusive rights or inclusion into resources. Both long and short-term goals were all ways to control whatever government was in power and if they weren't, laws were in place that would take years to change the present system. Sam had always understood these layers of intricacies that could be used to your advantage or at least know exactly what you're up against. At one-point years ago a budget with a police force was increased to look into missing persons of questionable character. This would not do in Sam's eyes. A few lobbying groups were contacted to create distractions and pull moneys from the missing persons team that had been set up.

Then during the next election, questions were raised by many groups on the distribution of police funding in general not particularly the missing persons. Questions were asked why there was funding going into areas where no visible crime had been committed. During the same time connections within newspapers began writing articles on organized crime. Others and I in the group were always amazed at how Sam could see both the angles and layers, two or three steps in advance. He was one of those rare men who very seldom ever said, "could have or would have." On occasion, he described how he organized the outcome of events. He would just consider more variables and more possibilities than most people. He described it as the main goal was the tree trunk, but how you got there was through the leaves and branches. If a followed trail ran out. He would just go to another branch that led in the same direction.

Then there was the list. This list comprised of three or four hundred names or abbreviations that you don't want to have recorded with any connection to you. The list hadn't been released to the public yet and probably wouldn't for another 10 or 15 years. These names were certain people, groups, gangs or organizations mostly involved with war or crime as well as some sorts of government agencies, others were for transportation or infrastructure. And then there were the abbreviations relating to weapons, chemical, biological or conventual, natural disasters, or disease outbreaks.

This was still only in the late '90s when very few people knew that every text, email, phone call or blog was being recorded and attached to people or IP addresses. Blanket searches could be used in this huge database or you could just specify an individual name attached to an IP address. That was enough to retrieve conversations or specific words for years at a time.

I had joked to Sam once, saying that with all the surveillance and information it's a surprise there's any crime at all. Sam already knew the answer, with a smile, violence produces fear, fear produces more laws, more laws create larger government organizations to implement them and enforce them. There was a balance, a ratio that had been worked out in the early 1900's. It has been refined through two World Wars to near perfection and is now implemented in every country in the world to control the population's and the masses. In the countries with the greater gross domestic product per person, the ratio of violence is usually lower accept in areas with low productivity, clusters you might call them. This is where the culling takes place. Countries of lower productivity ratio, the violence would be created by both government and individuals would be much greater.

The majority of all wealth in the world is generated by fifteen percent of the population, the "worker bees" you might call them. You've probably known some, or their types, hard working, honest with a high level of integrity with above average speed strength, quick learners. People usually able to work independently or entrepreneurial types. You always want to keep the ringers as in the top ten percent productive workers and racehorses, the people who were naturals but had not been fully developed yet. Then there's that large middle group that's helpful in lower-skilled jobs and maintenance work. The bottom twenty percent, well they would be either locked up or let out when needed or left to run free without punishment to create more crime and fear. Another alternative, in higher gross domestic countries they would be culled, put in jail or just made to disappear.

I was beginning to wonder if I shouldn't have

asked Sam about this section of files. Also, I hadn't even gotten around to asking him about the last file. Because that's when it starts to get strange. I read it three times just to make sure I wasn't misunderstanding something. Although it would explain things, that I've experienced over my lifetime. Such as myself experiencing as a child what was then called deja vu, or when ever I used the bathroom in our old family house that have been built in the forties, how I would fold out the two mirrors above the sink that were attached to the cabinet doors to a position that would reflect infinity copies of my own face by adjusting the doors slightly. I could increase or decrease the copies of myself. At the time I wondered why they looked exactly like me but, somehow weren't me.

The files contained records accumulated over thousands of years by scholars and seekers of truth. The words and symbols had been carved or molded into clay or stone with the intent to be passed to the next generations of seers for thousands of years. All this was not understood by the people who found them, until recent years when the Rosetta Stone was discovered and understood to be the tool for translation.

The universe was not a simple place or singular. It's not a coincidence when people come up to you and carry on a conversation as if they've known you for years, on another version of this world they have. Or sometimes when you meet a person and it feels like you already know them. What are the cities, towns or countries that you're drawn to and why? Why when you're there, it feels like home? When this happens at an older age, it's easy to just assume that you've seen a picture of it somewhere before. As a child, it's not as easy to explain, it is, as if you've seen that exact frame in time before, in a place you've never been to. The file goes into greater detail on meditation techniques to access consciousness of alternate realities of yourself.

Training consists of numerous different types of breathing techniques, some similar to those in yoga others unique to themselves. There is the visualization, upon awakening and before you fall asleep. The importance of regular eating of quality food along with exercise, increases likelihood of your mind recognizing events for what they are when they happen. The meridian lines that run around and through this planet have a slightly different vibrational sound then other parts of the planet. At different times of our life when traveling you might notice them. It's not unusual to see things or experience these vibrations, possibly as ringing in your ears. Or they may manifest themselves as turbulence on a plain, on a clear day with very little wind. Or a section of deserted road that feels like you are in a vacuum, no movement, sometimes even the light reflects differently off all objects.

As for myself, the first time I met myself I was

on a deserted road in the middle of the desert in 1986. There were now at least two versions of me that I knew of. Until reading this file I thought it was unique to me. It's not something you would discuss at a job interview.

Sam said it was obviously a long discussion. He referred to it as two different parts of his personality when he was younger. Understanding later in life, that what he was communicating with was separate persons in different realities. He began to use it as a tactical advantage when organizing the outcome of events throughout his life. The first time, he himself read the file, Sam was relieved to know he wasn't insane. People like himself throughout history had experienced exactly the same thing and took the time to document it for the benefit of others in the future.

The documents ended up falling in and out of the right and wrong hands many times over the centuries. The seers didn't actually need it to contact themselves, but it certainly helped explain things. When the tablets and records were in the wrong hands it was of no use. Without the natural ability it was very difficult to become a seer even with a life of training. The benefits of this were that over a few generations the interest in the text would be lost only to be found by other generations decades or centuries later. Persons with the natural ability would be drawn to it. The information and the practices are spread out over the entire planet. The people who do find it may not understand exactly what the attraction is but something within them draws them to the training or literature. In turn, like the group that had recruited Sam, recruited others like me.

It was only after Sam had been shown the file himself, that he understood that he was not alone. He started to begin his mornings and evenings with the meditations, visualization and breathing techniques described in the file. After a few years of practice, he understood that what he thought were parts of his own personality were in fact other versions of himself. They all existed in similar worlds to his own, but slightly different.

Whenever he was investigating more complex problems with variable outcomes, he consulted the group through his practiced meditations. Their lives were similar but not always the same timeline for events. Some had often tried and failed at the same plan. Others had succeeded with a different plan.

In the last few years some of the other versions of himself had started to disappear. He suspected that they had died of the same cancer that he had been diagnosed with. That was as much as he could tell me for now. Sam was tired, the cancer was taking its toll. I could see it in his eyes and hear it in his voice. Sam was not long for this world.

CHAPTER 8

The routine of physical labour has a few rewards such as a sense of accomplishment at the end of the day. At least when things go well, and it was one of those days. Sheila, my wife and a bit of a unicorn had planned a surprise. Honey garlic pork ribs and a fresh bottle of rum. Things were looking up. I had eaten my fill and was on my second rum. The kids were away for the weekend. Sheila was curled up on the couch with a cat like smile on her face when she brought up the subject of sex. I was thinking it doesn't get much better, ribs, rum and sex.

She brought up the subject of a colleague at work who had had breast augmentation. Noting that they were quite something. Jokingly I asked if she had seen them? She smiled and said yes, adding that they were amazing. Well I said, still being naughty and joking "when could I see them, for research purposes?" With another smile from Sheila, she said "why don't you ask her yourself". I was still chuckling to myself and appreciating my wife when the doorbell rang.

Never underestimate a unicorn, I answered

the door along with Sheila. We hadn't been expecting anyone. I should say I wasn't. It was my wife's colleague and friend Stacie. She was wearing a peasant girl dress and sandals. I had trouble saying hello and nice to meet you without staring. What I was staring at could only be described as two perfectly shaped ski slopes. I didn't know they were even able to do that with breast augmentation. Typically, they just look like a couple of balloons with nipples on them. But not these ones.

I was trying not to make it too obvious that I was staring. She didn't seem to mind or comment on it, just a little smile in the corners of her mouth and a lump forming in my pants. She joined us with a glass of red wine on the sectional. I think the wine was Apothic. My wife being coy, mentioned that she had invited Stacy for a drink after dinner and hoped I didn't mind. Then she said she had mentioned to me that she had had breast augmentation. I was kinda listening to this and wondering if it could get any better. Stacie still smiling says, "would you like to see them up close"? I'm like, "sure if it's okay with my wife?" My wife replies "sure it's okay with me', with a slow pat and rub on my inner thigh. Which she knows turns me on. As I'm turning back to Stacy, she had already slipped down the peasant dress to her waist. They were better than I had imagined, perfectly shaped slope with round full bottom curve. I think I was leaning in and around a bit to get a better look at this point.

Stacy then asked it I would like to touch them. I didn't ask for permission from my wife this time. As she was already leaning on me rubbing my inner thigh and crotch. My hands were up moving around them in awe. As Stacy leaned forward and kissed me slowly, my wife, the little unicorn, undid my pants and started giving me a blow job. I leaned back and let them have their way with me. Perfect breasts in my face and hands and a woman who knew me all to well down below. She knew I was getting ready to orgasm from years of experience. That's when she popped up and asked Stacy if she would like to finish me off. They then traded places, As I was orgasming, she whispered, "I hope you like the surprise".

I said I did and said, "I wouldn't want to underestimate you." She smiled, then we moved to the bedroom for the second and third rounds, with a few small breaks in between. One of the breaks involved a shower with two women. Slow wet and slippery, just the way I like it. I'm not sure how many times I was up and down along with them, but it seemed like more then a few. We dried off and headed back to the California king. I was as limp as a noodle and needed time to recover. Well, Sheila and Stacy were now squeaky clean and had something else in mind. I didn't mind watching. Women are a little more precise when making love to each other. Slow, more time spent on the details.

They were in a sixty-nine for quite a while. It was turning me on, but I wasn't quite sure when or how to jump in. Women move more slowly and are gentler, less rushed than men. But I suppose they also know the equipment better, perhaps even they're a little more aware of the subtleties and responses of the other. At some point they noticed that I was still beside them. Stacy moved around and slipped down between my wife's legs. Gently masturbating her and working her tongue against her clitoris. I moved towards my wife, first kissing her and then moving down towards her nipples, one free hand was caressing her stomach, the other, her breast, along with my tongue. Her eyes were dilated and her hips flowing to the rhythm. After few minutes she reached between my legs and started caressing my scrotum and cock. Increasing the rhythm, as life started to come back into it. The three of us we're now moving two some unseen ancient rhythm and beat. She pulled my now hard cock to her mouth and began sucking it and working it with her hand. I had one hand on her head and another on her breast lightly moving it in and out of her mouth. She gently pushed my hips away and nodded towards Stacey who was now up on her knees with her head still between Sheila's legs. I'm looking at Sheila's amazing ass as I plunged my now throbbing cock to her wet vagina. She began to moan along with my wife. We were all moving in the same direction and the same rhythm. I soon shuttered with what was my fourth orgasm in over three hours. Judging by the moans and sounds that were coming out of two women, I can only guess they both had also been satisfied. We laid down beside each other on the oversized bed. I cannot recall when, I had been so sexually satisfied in my life. We drifted off to sleep and I don't recall moving or dreaming at all that night.

I woke up the next morning to the smell of waffles and bacon. It just keeps getting better. There was a note beside the bed from Stacy thanking us for the amazing night and my wife for sharing her husband. I quickly showered, dressed and headed to the kitchen for that great smelling food. My wife was leaning over the stove looking smug and cute in her Japanese kimono. I gave her a quick peck on the cheek and sat down to a great breakfast. We talked about the night before and how it might affect us in the future. We were both pragmatic about it and had no regrets. She defined the word polyamorous; I had not heard of it before. They used to just call it an open marriage. Neither of us were sure that that was what we wanted but both agreed it was great experimenting, though we would not go out of our way, to join groups or other couples, but if something came along once in awhile and we both agreed to it, we were fine with that.

A month later my wife mentioned that Stacy had met a man and was in a monogamist relationship that was working out great. I guess there won't be any seconds on that.

CHAPTER 9

It had been five months since I had received a text from Janice. It seemed like a stretch, some had been longer, some shorter. The leaves were turning brown. The nights were clear and cool. Billy Ray the pedophile with thirty years of praying on young boys was finally getting out on early parole, thanks to the wonders of the Canadian Judicial System. He was described as a model prisoner. He would have to wear a monitor and report weekly to his probation officer. Billy Ray was to be housed just outside of Vancouver, in Burnaby British Columbia. It's easier to hide pedophiles in areas with larger populations. I had received his address along with the route he took to work. He had already started to get into a routine. He was a phone sales marketer. The bus stop was a few blocks from the half-way house. Then a twenty-minute ride to the exchange. To his delight, along this route was a coffee shop, right beside a daycare for toddlers, his favored prey. Legally, he couldn't be within 200 meters of a playground or school, but he could spend an hour here every day between catching buses, who would ever know?

He could fantasize about everything he

wanted to do and know one would know. Billy Ray started giving the observed toddlers pet names, like Seymour, Benge, and Dorothy. Oh, his favorite was Sinbad, a small south east Asian boy. While in the coffee shop, he had made lists of times and days when the parents or siblings dropped the children off. What Billy Ray didn't notice was the man sitting several tables away with his back to him, typing on his laptop, but not just any laptop. This one had a camera in the top corner of the screen instead of the middle. also programmed software that read lips. Most people weren't aware that when they think or talk to themselves that they tend to move their lips. Billy Ray was a lip mover, none stop. After a week of tracking this pedophile, it took all of Max Jobbers will, not to drop an axe in Billy Ray's head there and then. But that wasn't the way, patience, patience.

Once a week, I had started taking walks though Burnaby Central Park in the evenings, stopping at the duck pond where I liked to feed the birds. There would be less people around on a rainy day and the weather report was calling for rain this weekend. I had a time and place just the how too, to figure out. Two trails merged at the pond. A man in park maintenance coveralls pushing a garbage dolly wouldn't look out of place and could easily block the trail entrances with a work in progress sign after Billy Ray had entered.

Then there was the ankle bracelet, that

tracking device on Billy Ray's foot was a problem. That would need to be removed and put back in his apartment by 10 p.m. No need to alert anyone. Also, if it was left in his apartment it would appear that he was somehow able to remove it and skipped town. With a good quality short handled wood saw, I estimated it would take under a minute and a half to cut off his foot. Then between approaching him, breaking his neck then loading him in the dolly, I would need another three to four and a half minutes of privacy. I was starting to look forward to Friday and washing this piece of shit off the sidewalk.

Well Friday came along and it was one of those gray miserable days that you can get on the West Coast throughout the winter. The dampness in the air and constant drizzle are relentless. The dark cloud covered sky and absorbed all light. Another tracker had texted me that Billy Ray had left the house and was walking in this direction. I am pulled over to one of the far trail entrances and put up a work-in-progress sign. It was only a few minutes later while I was inspecting a garbage bin at the other entrance when Billy Ray walked by. I blocked the other entrance with a sign and some yellow tape. Taking my time, I walked towards the duck pond. Pushing the dolly along with me.

Billy Ray thought to himself, what another beautiful day and he certainly wasn't going to let a little rain get him down. He had made a new recipe for the ducks that he loved to feed them. It was like looking after little children, well someone had to look after them and he had so much love to give. Life was looking good. He thought he heard something behind him. What the fuck.

 Max Jobber was glad to see no one was around except Billy Ray feeding the ducks from the bench a few feet from the water.

I parked the dolly buy the garbage bin and quietly walked up behind him with my soft soled shoes. I could see Billy Ray cock his head, he probably heard a footstep, but it was too late. There was no chit chat, no discussion just a quick snap of Billy Ray's neck. Checking in both directions nothing appeared out of the ordinary. I quickly moved the dolly over, then cradling him like a child in my arms I lowered him into the bin. It was deadly quiet except for the drizzle of the rain. I quickly pulled out the saw and removed his left foot about four inches above the ankle bracelet. With his foot in one hand and the saw in the other a voice from behind me said, "vut are you up to"? I dropped the saw in the bin and slowly turned around with Billy Ray's left foot still in my hand. It was an elderly lady standing behind me, small frail looking with what I would consider beady little eyes. Without missing a beat, I told her I'd been stalking this man for a few years. He was a convicted pedophile and had recently been released from jail. I've broken his neck and now plan to dispose of his body. The elderly frail looking woman, looked me in the eye and said, "you are a good man", then walked away.

I covered his body and severed left foot up with a few loose bags, then retrieved the work-in-progress signs at both ends of the trail. It was easy to load the bin into the back of the van and tie it down. I didn't want it rolling around bumping into things. I had some cleaning products to wash off the ankle monitor. Then attached a note to it saying thanks for all the chicken, (code for young children among pedophiles). My associate had planted a few things around the house and in Billy Ray's laptop indicating that he done research on traveling to the new sex market for pedophiles in India. Mostly on account of Thailand which used to be his favorite had started chasing them out of their country by way of extradition with both Canada, the US and a variety of European countries. I had his keys to his apartment and without being noticed, entered the apartment and left the monitor on the kitchen table.

The rain had stopped, and the sky had begun to clear as I drove out of the city. By the time I got over the Port Mann Bridge, crossing the Fraser River, the moon was peeking out behind patches of cloud. Thirty minutes later I was on a rural farm road turning into a driveway of an old barn. I'd had access to this for storage. There was a storm drain in the middle of the floor that drained out to the Fraser River a few blocks away. The owner, an old friend had assured me, he had confirmed this years ago with some blue dye. The bin with the rubber lining was unloaded, placed over the drain and four one-gallon jugs of hydrofluoric acid were dumped on top of the body. After a cup of green tea and a tuna sandwich I checked on the progress of the decomposing body, it had only been 45 minutes, by prodding it with a with a long wooden stick I could tell most of the flesh and some of the bones had already liquefied. In another hour, I would start cutting the mix with water and draining it down the storm drain. I spent the next hour cleaning and bleaching the saw, my clothes and myself. I attached fine strainer to the end of the wooden stick. If confirmed that there were no solid materials left in the tote. Not that I'm a trophy collector, I would just dispose of them separately. I began adding water to the mixture cutting it by fifty percent, then opened the drain on the bottom of the tote. The soupy mixture slopped down the drain and out into the Fraser River. I continued hosing and washing the tote down along with misting it inside and out with a 50/50 bleach-water mixture. If anyone ever checked the drain and found anything, it would most likely be from the hundreds of deer that have been strung and butchered in the same spot.

CHAPTER 10

It seemed like a long day and a longer night. I had cleaned up, locked up the barn and was looking forward to the quiet drive home. But life had something else in mind for me that night. It was late 1:30 or 2 am in the morning, on what was a rainy night that had now cleared to a few scattered clouds. The back road I was on, that led to nowhere should have been empty and lifeless. I've driven the same road many times, not weekly or monthly but enough that I knew it. What I didn't recognize up ahead was a small restaurant attached to a building that looked to be 50 or 60 years old. The old weathered sign that was well-lit, read restaurant open, fresh coffee and homemade blueberry pie. I slowed, stopped and then pulled in as homemade blueberry pie is one of my favorites. I'm not sure how I could have missed this place over the years. It appeared to have old-style paned windows and a warm inviting feel to it. There were a few cars parked outside that all look like they belong there. There were six tables and maybe a dozen people sitting around along with one friendly waitress, all minding their own business. I eyed the only open seat left in the place.

It was a table for two with one of the seats occupied by someone who look just like me.

Jesus Christ it was me. I sat down with what probably looked like a *what the fuck* look on my face. What looked like my identical twin just had that five-mile stare and not much expression on his face. His first words were "how's it going and is this your first time"? I said, "going is getting a little strange and first time for what"? He nodded and the guy at the table beside us looked over, chuckled and said "newbie". My new identical twin then asked if I knew where I was? I smiled and said, "a restaurant on a country road." He smiled back, then said back to me, "is that really what you think this is"? I wasn't sure what was going on, but a coffee and some homemade blueberry pie appeared in front of me. He smiled and said, "don't try to eat or drink it". He then described where we actually were. It was a transit station or what you might call a crossroad, where other versions of yourself along with other species could interact. I was having trouble believing what he was saying, and things were only going to get stranger. He asked me to repeat these words three times, remove the veil, remove the veil, remove the veil. I did as he asked, more because I wanted to get to the blueberry pie then expecting something to happen. He then asked me to look more closely at the other people in the restaurant. The other people began to come and go in and out of focus. I described what I was seeing to him and thought it odd. He asked me to repeat the words again three times and continue looking at the other people. He piqued my curiosity, I did again as he asked. As I was watching, the people changed shape into something other than human. He began describing what I was seeing, these weren't humans but other species that had traveled to the same spot in space and time.

At the table next to me were two reptilian beings wearing uniforms, I could hear them both making clicking sounds with their throats and it seemed to be translated to an understandable language inside my mind. They seem to be talking about family and friends in particular making fun of someone what they both knew who was constantly getting into shit. Another two that I think were females, seemed to be of a plant-based species. They were in the shape of an hourglass but with heads arms and legs. Their surface was a light eggshell blue, but instead of eyes, ears or nose they had what looks like flowers coming out of where their eyes or mouth that would have been on humans. These were used for communication as sensors for their surroundings. Oddly enough I found them quite attractive. I was still curious about them when I walked up to one. She approached me and we were standing in front of each other. I'm not sure what type of communication took place, but she released a faint scent that was both pleasing and seductive. I noticed a lump forming in my pants. Which I found odd, on account of I was having my first contact with a plant that could communicate. I was told later that they release some sort of pheromone when encountering other species but were otherwise very friendly. I meant to ask him when he said, friendly as in a sexual way. But I thought I'd let that one slide. I smiled then headed back to the seat with my twin. The other group in the room were short, maybe four feet tall, thin boned with somewhat flat foreheads, with a unibrow. They seemed very animated when they spoke to each other. Hands moving, head moving up and down and sideways. Their teeth were pointy I assumed they were biters.

My twin Max looked like he was getting a little bored. I asked him how many times he had come to this place. He had lost count. We talked a bit about our current lives. His, was very similar to mine. By chance, I asked him if he'd ever been approached by a little old lady while he was in the middle of collecting a debt. He said "yeah and that she is called the traveler". She is singular throughout the Universe and her job seems to be to keep things in balance like a gardener. He had met her several times, and the conversations were always about the task at hand. She arrived and disappeared like a ghost. My twin considered her a friend but wondered if his name might appear on her list one day. Either way the next time I saw her I would ask more questions.

My twin Max went into more detail about what was available in this crossroads of space and time. When you entered the restaurant or portal, time appeared to continue at a normal pace. At this place, besides meeting other species, you had access to knowledge. You could spend years here studying with no sense of time passing. You did not age, there was no need for food or drink. Once you left the restaurant or portal you would enter back into your original space and time, as if no time had passed at all. To someone watching it would appear you just walked through the door then right back out. At some point when you enter the portal you could begin your real education. My twin Max had spent years studying other cultures, other species, along with languages, medicine, physics. It seemed to have a calming effect on him over the years, but also distanced himself from the people on his home planet. "You seem to have very little interest or chit chat with the other species" I asked my twin? He said over the years that he had been studying different cultures and languages and that he somehow lost his sense of humor. Most of the species seem to enjoy humor or at least a good story. I took a mental note to try not to fall into that trap.

I asked where these portals were located. He said they're spread around the planet. I recalled an experience I had had down in Baja Mexico years ago and asked if there were any portals in that area. He said yes, but they're a bit out of the way neither he nor the other species use them that often. There was some discussion on whether the restaurant or portal that I had come through was always visible. He said it wasn't, at least not too many. He then advised me to remember the words, remove the veil, remove the veil, remove the veil. With that he said goodbye, then slowly got up and walked out the door. I looked back down at my coffee and blueberry pie but what I saw was a controller for access to the great libraries. Looking around I noticed they were attached to each table for easy access by all. I spent the next few hours reading up on the physics of the platform crossroads that I was in. The first section was on the physical world, and the relationships between planets, stars, our solar system and our galaxy. I wasn't sure how long I was there for, but judging by the pages, descriptions and diagrams I thought it might have been a month or two. It was time for me to head back to my own world and my own time before I became too detached from it. I headed towards the door turned my head for one last look, nodded at one of the species I had become friendly with then headed out the door.

It was the same moonlit night that I left only a second ago. The roads were clear and had dried from the heavy rains. I made it back to my home, showered and crawled into bed beside my snoring wife.

CHAPTER 11

Back to the grind working 8:00am to 5:00pm six days a week. Pulling wrenches, filling out work invoices. Saturday afternoon, the last day of the shift it's always something to look forward to. There's always beer in the fridge that customers have dropped off as a thank you for getting their work done on time, and if there's not, there's always a bit of cash around to pick up a 24 pack. The guys always made sure the shop floor was washed, and most of the equipment wiped down and put away. I found these tasks always gave myself and employees a sense of accomplishment at the end of the week, just leaving the shop clean and ready for a fresh start Monday morning seemed to put most people in a good headspace. The jobs all went well that day and the beer was cold. Shooting the shit with men you work with and trust is always a pretty good way to end the week. This time would give us a chance to bitch about customers or laugh about a job that went for 'complete shit'. Those are the jobs that everything you touch falls apart or breaks in your hands. Something as simple as removing a bolt ends up being a four-hour job tapping and drilling out an exhaust stud broken in the engine head. Then there's always the joy of explaining it to the customer. A few of them would even ask who's going to pay for that? My answer was always the same. The owner of the truck pays for it. Then explaining that it's not a brand-new truck and that the repairs he spent on average over the year, are still cheaper than buying a new one. Warranty on a brand-new commercial truck is usually bumper to bumper for the first year or a hundred thousand miles. I often had customers asked how much it would cost to get that type of warranty on a used truck. My standard answer was the cost of a new truck, usually said with a shrug. Jim, Brad and Sean had all kicked out a lot of work this particular week. I acknowledged that, as I cracked open another beer and passed it over. It was one of those warm summer nights when no one was in a hurry to get home. It was also the weekend of the annual Air Show and we had watched dozens of flybys, by both the Blue Angels and the Snowbirds. At one point we had abandoned our jobs, got the ladder to climb up onto the roof of the shop to watch, for 20 or 30 minutes. It was worth it; it had boosted morale and did not affect productivity.

My cell phone rang, it was Janice, I haven't heard from her in a few months. She said Sam had passed away. He had lost his fight with cancer. The group would probably get together in the next week or so. She would advise me when the funeral was and where. I finished off my beer thanking the guys for a good day's work and with a smile reminded them to lock up and turn the alarm on.

I made it home and opened a bottle of Bourbon, I think it was Bulliet brand. I set two glasses out, One for me and one for Sam. The sun hadn't set yet and it was hanging low over the hills. We talked and drank most of the bottle, mostly me doing the talking. Sam was a quiet guy at the best of times. I decided I needed to clear my head and an hour run on the motorcycle through some winding roads would do the trick. I decided on the sport bike in the garage. a BMW R 1100S. It could do 260 kilometers an hour wide open; I didn't think I'd need any more than that. I pulled onto the freeway; it was about five kilometers from my turn off into the hills of Columbia Valley. The car beside me decided he wanted to race and so did I. We were already doing 110 kilometers an hour when we started, I had pulled ahead within a few seconds. When I look down to check my speed, the speedometer read 210 kilometers an hour, in the second that I looked down I had also come up on two cars side-by-side. I didn't have time to break at that speed, so I decided just to split them. In a normal state of mind, I would have slowed down after that, but I knew the turnoff was only two kilometers ahead and the road were clear ahead. The Bourbon was saying faster but I slowed down after the exit and returned to normal driving speeds. I wondered why my pulse hadn't increased or why I haven't even gotten an adrenaline rush. I weaved my way around the lake then up into the loop of Columbia Valley. It was dark by then, but the high beam light was more than enough to cover the road. I wondered what Sam would have said to me at taking a risk like that without the possibility of gaining anything. He always based his decisions on logic and common sense. Make every move count, waste as little time as possible, were some of his favorite sayings. I made it home safely that night only to wonder the next day what has gotten into me. I would miss him, and it would probably take a few years to get over that. Kind of like that damn Blue Heeler, Bullet. It's been seven years and I still think about that damn mutt.

For the next week I questioned my own mortality, my past, my present and the possible variations of my future. This seems to happen when close friends or people I've known for years die. I seem to recall the good times, the bad times and some of the funny shit that happened over the years with that person.

I remember being a kid, sixteen or seventeen years of age, when one of my aunts died. I recall her being a hard-drinking gregarious woman. She was quite a handful for my uncle, but I think he loved her. At the age of ten or eleven, I recall her driving me and her son, my cousin, who was about the same age, home. She had drunk so much she could barely drive. Those were the sixties and you could get away with that shit pretty easily. I was thinking about her and her life as I was driving away from the graveyard in my old beat-up 1966 Pontiac wondering almost out loud, word for word, was she going to go to heaven. At the same time, I reached down and turned on the radio. The first words that came out were "and she's walking the stairway to heaven" by Led Zeppelin. Still to this day it's kind of creepy.

CHAPTER 12

Sam's funeral was held in what I would call an estate. It was a large acreage with a historical stone house that had been added onto and updated. Someone with money and patience had put a lot of time and thought into this place. Sam being a practical man had been cremated. There was a broad spectrum of people attending, colleagues, friends, family and more than a few were serious looking. I recognized our crew, in particular Janice. As usual we couldn't acknowledge ourselves in public, just a slight nod and an acknowledgement of recognition. Words were said, by people who had known Sam for a lifetime. It was obvious Sam had gained the respect of all the people who were attending by thinking before he spoke or acted. He seemed to always be two steps ahead of the average person. I never had a chance to tell him I ran into his traveler friend Elizabeth. I thought I would remind him of the story he told me about the elderly lady and the knitting needle. I was heading out the door checking my pocket for my car keys. When I noticed there's a piece of paper with them that haven't been there before. It was a note from Janice, she had slipped it in without me knowing. She wanted to meet down the road at a hotel restaurant. I'm not sure where she learned how to do that, but she would have made a great pickpocket.

It was a classic older two-story well-maintained hotel with twenty rooms located on the second floor and a restaurant bar and banquet room on the ground floor. The restaurant was private in the back with a French door leading out to a garden patio.

Janice had been thinking about Max since the last time she saw him. Her home situation hasn't changed, and she felt she needed to look after herself once in awhile. Max was always a willing partner. The restaurant was known for quiet, fine dining, but was a little on the expensive side, it ensured privacy both among patrons and employees. She and others had conducted meetings and rendezvous here for 30 years. She was hoping for a nice lunch; maybe French onion soup and a light salad then head up into one of the rooms she had already rented to spend a few hours with Max. She checked her makeup and dress in the washroom before she sat down. She thought she was still looking pretty good. She'd had kept up with aerobics classes and yoga after high school and she thought the results showed. Her curves were still in the right places for a woman in her forties. Probably better than most. It always surprised her when she sees Max for the first time in weeks or months that her heart still flutters. She found it hard not to giggle to herself in anticipation. She was in a booth beside the patio and had a clear view of the entrance to the restaurant. Max had walked in the restaurant and spotted her immediately. With a slight smile he came to the booth, gave her a quick kiss on the cheek and slid in across from her. He looked a little tired, but she thought she could fix that.

Max liked the restaurant and the hotel. It was private and a hundred yards off the main road. He had heard of the hotel but had never been in it. It was easy to spot Janice at the far end in a private booth. He was hungry and looking for a good lunch with benefits. It always surprised him every time he saw her, how she looked as shapely and attractive as she did at 21. We talked a bit about what was going on in our lives and then, about Sam. Janice had been chosen by Sam to oversee the crew, as in myself and others. We all had complete trust in her and thought she was the best choice for many reasons. Janice recommended the French onion soup along with that I ordered a baron of beef dip. She also had a French onion soup but with a beet spinach salad on the side. I washed it down with a draft beer and her with a glass of cabernet. We talked for a while longer then reached across the table for our first real kiss. As usual a lump was forming in my pants whenever I touched her. The familiar peaches and Jasmine was running through my mind. She had already booked a room as I suspected, I couldn't get up there fast enough.

The room was classic and quaint, comfort that had been recently updated. In particular a high-end bed and linen. We kissed again as soon as we got in the room. Only this time more passionately, she sighed and relaxed in my arms. I could feel her nipples already poking through her blouse. Her hand was down in my pants working my cock with the expertise of a mature woman. We were now on the couch exploring each other as if it was the first time. I undid her blouse and bra and was now handling those large perfect breasts. She had unbuckled my belt and zipped down my zipper, allowing for all the room she needed. She put her head between my legs and started working it with her mouth. Only for a minute or two, I think she wanted to tease me. By this time, I had reached over, hiked up first skirt and removed her underwear. She came up for another kiss them turned around on the couch moving her knees to the ground rubbing her beautiful ass against my crotch. It didn't take much more encouragement as I mounted her from behind. Her smooth fleshy ass was bouncing around with moans of delight within a couple of minutes, I was orgasming. I collapsed onto her back breathing heavily. She rolled back around and pulled my head into those beautiful breasts. I continued with my mouth on her nipples that were now fully erected. As she thrust her hips against my lower ribs. I slipped my hand and finger between her legs adding a second finger and pulsating it into her vagina. She was moaning and thrusting her hips to the rhythm of my finger when she said "more". I added a third finger and continued working it rhythmically along with her breasts. She pushed my head down to meet my hand between her legs. Now normally I like to clean things up, but the passion was overwhelming. I began working her with my tongue and finger at the same time. The moaning increased along with her grip of her fingers in my hair. I'm not sure how long I was down there, but at some point, she slowed down, I came to a stop and lifted my head up to her face with a smile. Then she said it was time for a shower. I agreed with some relief and we headed into the bathroom.

While I tell ya, there's nothing like a slippery shapely woman in the shower all suds up. I didn't think I was up for seconds but apparently, I was, and it was great. We dried off and moved to the bed or what I thought would just be a cuddle and a short snooze. Who doesn't like a little snooze after great sex? Janice apparently had something else in mind. It surprised me how much of a nymph she can be when she wants to turn it on. She started with just her fingers playing along my chest and abs. Then moving down to between my legs. Of course, I was fine with this, but wasn't expecting any movement down there. Within a few minutes she also moved her head and along with the hand started working it. To my surprise some movement started. She was a passionate woman and knew how to work it. I was surprised that I was fully erect in 10 minutes. She straddled on top of me working her hips up and down with strength and flexibility. She leaned into me while one of my hands were caressing her ass and another on a beautiful breast allowing the nipple to slide into my mouth. With a free hand she reached behind herself, between my legs and started caressing my balls. I'm not sure how long this went on for, but I soon erupted for the third time in two hours. I slowed down along with her and she dismounted me. With a smile she asked if I had orgasmed, of course, I had, noting that it was for the third time.

My body felt lean and taunt, like that of an athlete. She was still laying beside me with a smile on her face playing with my chest hair on my chest with one hand. We might have both dozed off for half an hour or so but unfortunately like most people we had things to do and places to be. We both dressed, then as she was leaving, she said, we have a nasty one coming up be careful when you're collecting the debt.

Very few times had I seen such seriousness in Janice's eyes. This was one of those times and I took note.

CHAPTER 13

By his own account Khon had killed at least 500 girls or women. He had been working the human trafficking in India for eight years and it had begun to take its toll. At first, he was just the bait to lure girls from small towns. Usually poor uneducated and Muslim. The families were always eager to send them off with the handsome well-spoken young man. Within six months he had procured over a hundred young girls to be sold into prostitution. Khon understood very quickly where the money was, and that was managing the young girls both upstream and down. He had been brought up in the Dharavi slums of Mumbai, a son of a whore with no father. His mother had rented him out to homosexuals and pedophiles at a young age for the equivalent of five dollars a day. The only reason he survived was because of the strict rules of his mother's keeper, such as if you injured the merchandise you would be cut. That was the vicious animal Mohinder, he always kept his word and had demonstrated it on many occasions. The market of renting out young children to foreigners was booming. Thailand had agreed to extradition of all sex offenders to their country of origin. Thank God, India had no such extradition treaties with other countries. Praise to India. By the age of twelve years, Khon was considered too old for the pedophiles. His mother had died a few years earlier and he was then taken in by a boarding school run by nuns. They were almost as vicious as Mohinder, with daily whippings for the slightest indiscretion, but they fed, clothed and educated him. They quickly taught him to read and write along with English and math. By the age of sixteen, he was well read and spoken.

In the slums, most people knew other people's business. Mohinder had a new plan for attracting women into the trade. Khon was selling used cell phones in a small booth for a few dollars a day. Mohinder approached him with his plan. He thought Khon, with good looks and mild manners could be used as bait to attract young women with the offer of marriage. Mohinder thought they could both make hundreds of dollars a month in this new enterprise. Khon took to it like a duck to water.

Khon's wives or what were thought to be his future wives, were sold or put into brothels managed by Mohinder. The business was thriving but as expected in any business there were bumps along the way. The women were not willing participants and quite often put up a fight or tried to escape. The first few times of disobedience, they would be beaten or drugged, as a last measure they were killed and buried. Khon would usually just use a garrote wrapped around their neck. It was quiet and simple-to-use method of killing. For a few rupees, two men would show up and dispose of the body. The killing never bother him, it was just survival. He was protected by the local police that had been paid off. He never grieved or felt any remorse. Thinking back even when his mother was found dead in her room, he could not recall shedding a tear. After a while, the women's faces all seem to become the same face. He would sometimes try to recall more details about them but the only thing he would see was a collage of their combined features. Sometimes the family members would come looking for them. He would always just say they ran off or had met someone else and left him. He moved from place to place, never spending more than a day or two in one flat. It was after two years that he decided to get rid of Mohinder. He had built up his own crew and network of contacts and there would be no problem taking over the brothels.

Months became years and years had become seven, his lucky number. Life in Mumbai was becoming too high of a risk for Khon. Word had begun to spread over the last year of the hundreds of murders he had committed. Along with thousands of girls and women he had sold into a life of prostitution. There had been numerous attempts on his life both by family members of his victims and competitors. It was time to start up fresh somewhere else. One of his distant relatives was now a third-generation Canadian. They had reunited through Facebook and he has been convinced to immigrate to Canada and start a new life. The few things they knew about him was that he had saved enough money up to emigrate and that he had run a small phone repair and service shop in one of the worst slums of Mumbai. For Khon, it was easy enough to change his name. Any type of documentation could be easily bought in India: passports, driver's licenses, degrees from ivy league universities. None of them would hold up under heavy scrutiny but certainly good enough to get by Canadian immigration. Especially if you could demonstrate financial security and sponsorship. His relatives in western Canada had written glowing reference letters to his character along with his intent to start a small cell phone service outlet in the British Columbian communities of Abbotsford and Surrey.

What he didn't know about his newfound relatives in Canada was that the first generation were hard-working farm laborers who had then become farm owners. The second generation having had to work the land when they were kids and adults, now had very little interest in it, other than making the highest profits possible. Commonly, laborers on the farm were now Guatemalans who only worked seasonally and had no interest in staying in the cold hostile climate. The third generation of Indian Canadians were now involved with gangs and drugs, which both the parents and grandparents were proud of. It's a cultural thing. One of the past times of the third generation was to gang rape white girls after drugging them at parties and filming it, then passing the video around to friends before selling it on the dark web. Small video and cell phone repair stores were fronts for several things. One being the theft of ID and personal information off the phones that were supposed to be repaired, the other was using the stores as a front for laundering drug money.

Third generation Canadian East Indians, Khon's relatives were very excited about bringing their relative from Mumbai over to Canada to help him start a new life. They were sure they could work him like a dog and make much money off the naive Khon. They had brought over other kinsman do work in the field's years earlier but most of them lost the taste for it and they ended up driving trucks. Always laughing and reminiscing about the good old days before_9/11. Trucking was very profitable along the Golden Triangle back then. They would fill up their reefer vans with hydroponic pot along with their regular load and transport it from the Fraser Valley to Los Angeles. Once in Los Angeles, the drugs would be removed, their load of goods would barely cover their fuel costs. But the drugs made up for it. They would them pick up another load and head to Montreal, usually vegetables from the Sunshine State along with hard drugs, heroin or cocaine. These drugs would be dropped off in Montreal and if they could find a load to head back to Vancouver they would, otherwise they would run back empty. On paper the run would look like they barely broke even. But the 25,000 US cash they made off the little extras, more than made up for it. Quite often, the process involved the setup of an East Indian who had just gotten off the boat with a class one driver's license. Also utilizing two drivers per round trip so they could do the route in half the time. Telling the new guy that they were training him, and he should be thankful. This also gave them an ignorant patsy to take the fall should the truck be caught. If you were caught smuggling it will get you seven years in a federal penitentiary in the US. In Canada, well you might do a short probation. The drug running had been cleared by politicians pushing through lenient laws years earlier. Telling us all, you're not real criminals and one day it's going to be legalized anyways. All those lenient laws being passed were going to save us all tax dollars, was said by local politicians with a smile and a reassuring nod.

His new cousin had talked with Khon several times about his ability to extract information and personal data off cell phones.

Khon being well-spoken in both Hindi and English was a little surprised about questions regarding extracting data from cell phones. He just assumed these backward hillbillies, old school East Indians in the small farming community of Abbotsford had no idea how the world really works. They had sent him photos of their homes and cars, also, of the extravagant weddings. He was surprised there was that much money to be made in rural farms. They had said they usually grow blueberries or strawberries. He knew what these berries were but had never had one. As is with most Indians, he had noted a somewhat dim look in their eyes, similar to that of the Muslim families he had taken hundreds of brides-to-be from. They all looked chubby, soft and slow probably from living unventured lives. Khon could already tell it would be difficult not to take advantage of them.

CHAPTER 14

Dana Busham the newly recruited Iranian into the debt collectors' group had been contacted by members of the Muslim Brotherhood located in Mumbai. It had come to their attention a year ago that a Hindi, an Indian from the Dharavi slums was abducting young Muslim women or girls from rural communities and selling them into prostitution or human trafficking. It was suspected dozens had been murdered when they attempted to escape. They had made several attempts on his life recently but had failed. Mainly due to the close-knit interactions within the slum community. The general attitude of the inhabitants of the Dharavi slums was to live and let live. If they did not try to protect themselves within the slum, they would have no protection at all. Even though it was well-known that Khon was an animal and surely deserve to die they would prefer it was done elsewhere.

The Brotherhood have received information that Khon had been issued a passport and would be immigrating to Canada. The Muslim Brotherhood normally only targeted westerners and their infrastructure through legal means but on this occasion a non-Muslim was directly targeting the Muslim population. They had sent out a call through on the dark web about Khons new name and his sponsor's address in Abbotsford British Columbia. To Dana's surprise, while he was reading his weekly updates, Khon would be moving into his own backyard or to say hunting grounds.

Dana Busham would be considered a very moderate Muslim, for the people who knew him, they might not even know he was a Muslim. After seeing his own family and people of other religions murdered in his home country as a child, he had taken an oath to himself to protect all. He felt honored when Sam had approached him asking if he had an interest contributing to society on a much deeper level. A level most people don't have the stomach or character for, without ever receiving recognition or financial reward. He was thinking about this when he contacted Janice with the details of the information. He knew it would be turned over to Max Jobber but had asked Janice on this occasion that he would like to be more involved, as in hands-on. Explaining to her that he felt very passionate about this, as it resembled atrocities that had been committed in his own country by similar types of people in the name of the Shaw. He was also familiar with the local Indy population and he had a plan. Dana thought that with the right words spilled into certain ears that they could also start a gang war within the different criminal factions locally. He was well aware that the local East Indians in the Lower Mainland had branched out into drug smuggling and extortion. Normally their group, "the collectors" did not get involved in minor infractions such as drug smuggling or extortion within the criminal organization. However, in the last year, groups of young East Indian boys and men have begun gang raping young girls after drugging them at parties. The local police had been hiding this fact from the general population for over a year and a half. It was believed by some that this indiscretion of withholding the details of crimes committed by immigrants and minorities was better left undiscussed. There were certain individuals in at Federal and Provincial level police departments and government that had an agenda to push the ideals of the political far left-wing.

The sun was setting as Khon arrived from the East over British Columbia into Vancouver. He was amazed at the beauty and the lush forests around the city. It looked unnaturally clean and organized. He wondered to himself of how many peasants it would take to maintain such a city in this state. It was surprising how easily he moved through Canadian customs. He'd been coached on what to say to every question they asked. His paperwork was perfect along with his clothing and demeanor. The young female Customs officer that was checking through his paperwork would have fetched top dollar back in Mumbai, he thought to himself. Her shapely hips, smooth complexion with long eyelashes are all sought-after attributes.

Susan Charles, the Customs agent working her last hour of her four 12-hour shifts, thought the handsome East Indian was unusually well spoken in both English and Hindi as she read through his paperwork. He had that shyness and vulnerability about him that most women would find attractive. As he was walking away, she thought she remembered something. It was regarding the last name of the sponsorship family, Grawal or Grewal, Susan thought she remembered it from the newspaper three or four years earlier maybe longer. She was tired and the next traveler was waiting at her booth impatiently. What she didn't recall from the paper was that family name was involved in numerous murders and wife burnings that had occurred along the banks of the Fraser River over a ten- or fifteen-year time frame. Most of these crimes had been difficult to prove but family members had been sent to prison and now their relatives were waiting outside in the reception area for Khon.

CHAPTER 15

Three Grewal family members were waiting for Khon. Two were third generation Canadians, Steve and Harp, also their uncle Sanjeet who was second generation and who had done five years in jail for suspected involvement in a murder. Sanjeet had never married and he was known by relatives as being dirty, as in sticking his cock into anything, boys, men and the odd animal. Also, women when he could get his hands on them, but most women who knew him would have nothing to do with him, Indian or white. It's acceptable within the Punjabi community for unmarried men to engage in sex with each other. In most cases it's considered a bit of a joke when you tell people you're not married. Steven and Harp were both in their twenties. They had been involved with sports in high school now they mostly hit the gym just to stay toned. Harp had studied photography in high school then had taken a few courses at the local University. Where he made his money was from people watching his gang rape videos on the dark Web.

One of the more recent movies he had done was doing quite well, pulling in a thousand or two thousand dollars a month just from the high volume of viewing. He and Steve had headed out to the local nightclub with a couple of younger friends. They were well-dressed and well-groomed flashing the bling and the cash. It wasn't hard for them to start chatting up the table of girls beside them. Two of the girls were locals and the other two were in town with a women's softball team. The men had bought them drinks most of the night and then had talked them into coming back to their house for a few more. The two local girls declined but the other two from out of town thought, what the heck, these are nice guys. They had only had a drink or two at the home of these handsome men when they started to feel a little off. They were having trouble focusing when they thought they saw more people enter the room smiling and laughing. Susie the older of the two girls remembered someone trying to kiss her as she was pushing him away. Both girls woke up in their car in the hotel parking lot the next day feeling sore and wet down there. They were so groggy, that they barely made it into the hotel, showered then fell asleep for the rest of the day.

What they didn't remember was being gang raped by eight men and filmed. They had been slipped the well-known date rape drug Rohypenol, it was both colorless and odorless when mixed into a liquid. Then had their clothes removed. Susie had just been bent over on a waist height table well the men lined up behind her. Harp with his HD camera moved around the basement swiftly getting the best shots possible. At one point the excitement overwhelmed him. To relieve himself, he slid Susie's head to the side of the table and began masturbating into her mouth. He could hear the odd choking sound from her but was sure she was fine, maybe even enjoying it. Dirty Sanjeet of course wanted close-ups of his favorite act that was usually performed on men or animals. Steve had been nominated earlier to do the cleanup after an hour or so, most of the men had left. Thanking Steven and Harp for the entertainment, Sanjeet wiped the girls off with a warm wet cloth and took his time dressing them. He wasn't sure why but dressing women while they were unconscious always made him feel like a man in control of his life. They moved the women back to their car and drove it to their hotel parking lot that they had asked about earlier. They would sleep off the date rape drug in the safety of the parking lot probably not remembering anything that happened and if they did who would believe their story.

Khon immediately identified the three men with the card and his name written on it. They were well-dressed and appeared relaxed and happy to see him. Having grown up speaking Hindi, he, Khon was also familiar with Punjabi, but it was not commonly spoken throughout the country. He had no problem conversing with them in Punjabi or English. Khon felt something, he wasn't sure what it was, but his instincts had helped him to survive in the very brutal slums of Mumbai. The feeling was, he was being watched by someone other than the people he was with. He would have to acquire a weapon as soon as possible. The car they were driving was magnificent. He had never been in or seen one of this make and model. It was a white Escalade that comfortably sat seven people. They had set him up in the house with Sanjeet, in a small suite consisting of a bedroom with a sitting room. Meals of course would be with the family. Khon recognized the music playing on the vehicle sound system, as a popular Hindi pop band. Khon was entranced looking out the window of the SUV as it travels along Vancouver's streets. The cleanliness and the efficiency of the highway was something he had never experienced before. After an hour of listening to his cousins telling him about his new home he was still amazed by the roads and clean sidewalks also the mostly well-kept lawns of the suburb they pulled into. There were at least a dozen people at the home to greet him when he arrived. He started to wonder if any of them even worked. When he asked one of his cousins how they could possibly afford all this? With a laugh Steve and Harp said "Shiva provides for them" jokingly.

Dana Bushman looked perfectly at home and relaxed while he waited in the background of the airport's international arrival area. He wanted to observe the interactions between Khon and his new Canadian cousins firsthand. Reading about people or looking at photographs is not the same is standing beside them, eave dropping on their idle conversations. It's easier to see the hierarchy within the group when you're observing people interacting. Who were the leaders and who are the followers? When he first observed Khon walking towards them, he felt a rage inside of himself but only a fool or a Martyr would start shooting people in an airport. Dana Bushman was neither. He made his way back to his car and waited for them to pull out. He gave them lots of room on the road. There wasn't any need to follow too closely. Dana had been tracking their phones and knew where they were going. He pulled past the newer three storied houses, where Khon would be staying with Sanjeet, five minutes after they had arrived. His eyes may have moved around but not his head, not even for a glance. He had mounted cameras pointing towards the front and back on his car that would record all license plates that he could look up later.

CHAPTER 16

In Dana's home country of Iran, during the revolution when the Shah took power, they had pitted tribes and clans against each other by way of misinformation. Dana thought that they could use the same strategy to target the two gangs within the Indo-Canadian population on the West Coast. Not only would this clean up their immediate targets, Khon, Sanjeet, Steve and Harp, it would create animosity within the gangs that would require retaliations on both sides. With their groups ability to plant information on social media boasting about this or their targets on either side. This would assure years worth of conflict and the deaths of numerous gang members without lifting a finger.

Dana had located a stash of guns belonging to one of the gang members. The guns had been used in previous drive-by shootings and could easily be traced back to them. This information would then be leaked to the news and the general public. Assuring retaliation for the attack. Max Jobber certainly couldn't pass for an East Indian and would have to remain across the street or perhaps hidden in the backyard. Dana was sure he could handle three or four of them in the tight quarters of the basement's suite. With Max on the outside he could be sure that no one would approach him from behind. Max was not one hundred percent sure of the plan, mostly because he didn't like leaving any evidence. Just another missing person was always his preference. After a few weeks of discussion and studying of the logistics, working out of the who, how and where had been decided. It was just the when left, and they needed to have patience. They wanted to build a story along with threats, possibly some physical altercations within the Indo-Canadian community.

Khon had been introduced to two more cousins and distant relatives. He was facing the street looking through a large bay window listening to is cousins talk about the cell phone repair shops they had throughout the suburbs of Vancouver. The street was quiet with a very little traffic moving by the house. A grey four door sedan with a lone occupant, who did not even turn his head to look at the six or seven cars parked in driveway passed by. The driver appeared to have more middle eastern features then east Indian. He turned his attention back to his cousin and began inquiring as to the profit margins on what he considered inexpensive phones. His cousin Steve gave him a quizzical look as if he did not understand meanings of profit margins. Steve's understanding of markups and repair cost seem to be very limited. The monies he said that the shops generated had to be exaggerated or a lie. No one would wish to have a phone repaired at five or ten times the cost to replace it with a new one. He was pretty sure he could make his own assessment within a day or two of working at one of the businesses. He was tired and excused himself from the party. Then headed to his bedroom for some privacy. When he was in the privacy of his bedroom, he connected to the internet Wi-Fi through his laptop. He been given a contact in Canada to purchase a gun and switchblade from. He paid for the weapons through his International account and had them sent to the post office a few kilometers away from the house he was staying up. Khon had a dreamless night, waking up drenched in a cold sweat at 3 a.m. in the morning, exactly 3 a.m. He wondered if it was some sort of omen. He got up and walked around the basement, listening to the sounds of his new home. It was so quiet, and the streets were empty, something he had never experienced before. A sense of isolation and loneliness washed over him. He walked out the basement door standing quietly alone under the balcony. The air was fresh and clean. It dried the sweat off his body within minutes. He still felt uneasy much like before the attacks on his life in Mumbai. He reassured himself he was safe in this new land with these new people, just as his mother had reassured him when he was a child before sending him out with a new customer.

At breakfast Khon had never seen people eat so much, as these people did. It was no wonder that they all had a layer of fat on them. Like animals that are force-fed a month before slaughter. Khon was glad to get out of the house with Harp and spend a day at the cell phone repair shop. It was a small shop with a display area along with a cashier counter. The back room was where the phones were repaired, but it didn't look like much repairing was done. A few customers an hour would come in after some discussion with a low quote on labor they would leave their phone for a day or two to have the technician check it out. Harp would carefully write down the password of the customer's phone along with a home phone number that they could be contacted at. The phone was then handed off to a tech in the back room. The first thing they would do is scan the list of contacts within the phone and emails. Then they would download all emails that have not been deleted. If they had not been able to locate bank accounts, credit card numbers by then, they would phone the customer and ask for the Microsoft account or Google account passwords. This would usually give them access to the individuals bank accounts, PayPal and any online ordering by credit cards. Khon was now smiling in amazement at how these backwards hillbillies had come up with this, while he had not. Parm, the technician, looked up at him while he was in the middle of copying some sensitive data. Parm could tell by the look and demeanor of Khon that he knew exactly what Parm was doing. Khon nodded to him and commented that this data would be valuable information in India. Parm nodded back and thought to himself that Khon was going to fit into this lifestyle like a warm hand into a bucket of soft grease.

It had been a couple of months since Steve and Harp had picked up any girls for dirty Sanjeet. He had started to bug them about it and also noted that the revenues from the videos was decreasing. They needed new material. They discussed it with Khon noting that his good looks and shyness might help with picking them up. Khon didn't say it but, if the women or girls gave them any trouble, he would be happy to beat them or kill them. What the Grewal's didn't know was that their phones were being tapped and used as bugs to record what they were saying at a distance of thirty or forty feet even when they were not in use. Keywords triggered messages that were sent into databases, this had alerted both Dana Bushman and Max Jobber of their intentions on next Saturday night.

Khon had very little interest in sex but thought that he would enjoy the seduction, filming and rape. He was very pleased with himself that no one had noticed the gun that he now carried with him in his ankle strap along with this high-quality steel push dagger tucked in his pants. He learned to defend himself from his mother's keeper, also he had been taught to fight. Not as a sport, but only with the intent to cripple or injure the opponent. His main asset had always been his demeanor. Most people just assumed he was non-confrontational or submissive. His face showed little or no expression. Just his eyes, his eyes would always look through you rather than at you. His face could not be read and he'd learned the right words to say to put people at ease when they questioned him as to his intentions over the years. He had identified the difference between posturing and actual intent of injury at a young age. Khon had surprised people as a teenager after he'd been found standing over and injured or crippled person with little or no expression on his face. At the time he had said he was just trying to protect himself, which in most cases was true. Later he used those skills to terrify his competitors and the women that he controlled.

Steve had paid several bartenders at different clubs in town to keep an eye out for tables of women who might be from out of town and to reserve a table beside them for him and his crew. The bartenders would be tipped handsomely as soon as the Indian crew got there. This particular night, Steve got the call about 9:30 p.m. They hit the road right away looking and smelling like three happening dudes with money. As planned, they found themselves sitting beside three Finnish exchange students. The exchange students had finished their semester and were partying it up. Expecting to head back home in two days to work for the summer. It always surprised Steve and Harp, how gullible northern European women were. They have no idea how the other ninety percent of the world really lived. The men had ordered round after round of vodka shots. Steve reminded the waiter to put Grey Goose in the girls and water in theirs, by midnight the party was full on. They began to make the move to get the girls to come back to the basement suite. The girls adamantly said, "no", adding they didn't know them well enough. Cunningly, a single statement," that it was because they have brown skin wasn't it" was all it took to change the girl's minds. Now the students felt they had to prove that they were liberal and accepting of all cultures. They certainly weren't of their parents' culture and they would prove it by their acceptance of cultural, religious and ethnic differences. They thought it would be quite an adventure. What could go wrong in a small Canadian town?

CHAPTER 17

Max and Dana had taken their time listening to the recordings and watching the files. Like most criminals the Grewal's had overestimated their skills. Thinking they had been working in a closely-knit community with complete immunity. The car they were driving had a tracker on it. It didn't get any easier to follow then that, like shooting fish in a barrel Max said. Dana had no Idea what he was talking about, but just nodded. The tracker led them to the bar that the waiter had phoned the Grewal's from. Dana walked into the bar a few hours after the Indians arrived. He made a quick assessment and was sure tonight was the night. The group of women at the table beside them were young, possibly students. Dana was sure it was going down tonight.

Dana and Max went back to wait in an inconspicuous spot in a sport complex a few hundred yards from the house's driveway. At twelve fifteen am, the SUV pulled into the driveway with a four-door sedan behind it. Three men were in the SUV and three young women got out of the sedan. They all moved into the house. Max and Dana could hear light happy chatter as drinks were being passed around. Using Steve's and Parm's phones as listening devices was working like a charm. Within fifteen minutes of arriving at the house, the young women would be unconscious. Steve sent a text to who he thought was Harpreet, this text was intercepted, then answered by a third party, namely Janice, that the crew was on there way to the house. ETA of fifteen or twenty minutes.

It was now time for Dana to make his move. He had his vest on with a hoodie and jeans. Along with a nine-millimeter suppressed Glock. It was a dark cloud covered night with very little traffic on the road. He skipped up the driveway to the front door. Dana considered knocking but instead thought he would try it first. They were expecting more people, no need to lock it. What he saw when he walked through the door was one of the students passed out on the couch, along with another, who was half-dressed being loaded on a bed by Steve and Harp. Dana walked into the room behind them before they knew he was there. He shot them both in the back of the head. Two down one to go. What Dana didn't know, was that Khon was in the next room filming himself raping one of the unconscious girls.

Dana moved quickly to the next door expecting that Khon would not have heard the shots, unfortunately Khon had, the moment he stepped out of the door Khon was waiting with a gun in his hand, pants still around his ankles. One quick shot with the snub nose Smith and Wesson semi auto hit Dana in the side of the stomach but on the vest, spinning him back into the bedroom. He was paralyzed momentarily, but was able to yell, "back up, back up!" Khon followed him into the room shooting Dana twice in the chest before turning to run out the back door, not wanting to be around when the body was found by his relatives or the police. Fortunately for Dana, Khon didn't know Dana had a Kevlar vest on with a chest trauma plate.

Max had heard the first shot and was running for the house when the call for backup came through the earpiece. He considered going through the front door but decided to head along the side of the house to the back door. As he turned the corner at the back of the house, Max was shot point blank twice in the chest. The impact knocked him to the ground along with the air out of his lungs, looking up from the ground he heard a click. Khon's gun had jammed. Khon with the same calmness he had displayed during other altercations just squatted down on Max's chest pinning his arms with his knees. Khon brushed Max's gun away then pistol whipped him with his own jammed gun. Taking his time, he then pulled his push dagger out of his waistband, raising it above his head. Max was stunned but not out. He prepared to parry the knife and roll Khon over. But the blow never came. At the height of the ark he seemed to stop, then his body shuttered, arms dropping loosely to his sides. Max rolled him off easily. To Max's amazement the elderly women Elizabeth was now standing at his feet wiping a round pointed eight-inch rod off with a doily before placing it back into her purse. Looking at the blood coming from the back of Khon's skull, he realized she had thrust it into the back of his head just above the spine. Probably swirling it a couple of times to turn his brain into jelly, then pulling it back out. While pointing her somewhat withered crooked finger she said in an accented voice," you are getting sloppy, you were warned to be careful about this one. I don't have time to be following you around every time you decide to do something."

Dana had staggered out of the back door by this time. Seeing an elderly woman of perhaps northern European descent standing there along with Khon lifeless body was somewhat of a surprise. She seemed to be scolding Max with her wrinkled fore finger. Dana would have found this more amusing in another situation. With a quick glance at Khon, his only question was, "is he dead"? Max nodded and said, "very". Dana still holding his stomach, warily eyed the elderly woman, managed to ask who she was and then hastened Max to get there asses out of there. Dana helped Max up, then turned to ask the woman if she needed a ride but Elizabeth was gone, as if into thin air. They were now helping carry each other across the street. They would both recover with nothing more than a few stitches and a headache. Dana began asking as they were getting into the car," who the hell was that old lady." Max holding his sleeve to his head too stop the bleeding just said," it's a long story"

The police arrived within seven minutes in two different vehicles, alerted by calls about shots fired. They did a quick sweep of the premises. Finding two dead men with wounds to their head. They called for backup along with forensics Detectives. The women appeared unconscious but okay. They weren't sure what had happened, this would take time to sort out.

There was one woman undressed on a bed with a video camera sitting beside her. Another half dressed in a different room with the bodies, two more passed out on the couch. A sweep around the house found the body of a third man. Dead with a small amount of blood on the back of his neck. Dogs were brought in along with forensic detectives to do a thorough inspection of the area. The dogs did track a scent down the driveway and across the street to a parking lot, but it was lost after that. During the sweep one of the head detectives had opened a small shed in the backyard to find a goat tied up in a pen. The goat was cute by goat standards and quite friendly. He thought the rectangular box beside the pen was a little out of place. Perhaps it was used for grooming. He took a few photos for later reference. One of the forensic officers had picked up the video camera on the bed, rewound it and played the video. The man raping the unconscious women on the bed appeared to have the same pants and shoes as the dead guy outside. A quick check found a dozen other video files.

The ambulances had loaded up the girls to take to the hospital. The three bodies went off to the morgue for autopsies. Three murders in one night would be considered excessive even in the East Indian community. The officers spent the next day canvassing the neighborhood for information. They did not receive a single tip, no one was talking. The phones were checked by the forensic team. They had traced emails and phone calls for the last month. The videos were all date marked within the camera which matched up exactly with when they have contacted other individuals to come by the basement suite. The videos clearly showed dozens of different individuals involved with the gang rapes over the last year and a half. The investigation soon spread to the contact list on Steve and Harps phones. When the investigation began searching for those individuals, it was found that all of them that could be identified had left for extended vacations back to India.

Harp's phone had been synced with his computer and a cloud-based app, when the history was checked for web searches one site came up numerous times on a regular basis. It was a site located on the dark web and used for downloading videos. Within a few days the tech checking the site began to recognize the individuals in the rape scene footage. With access to Harps account on this website, they were able to see both downloads and uploads. Harp had received hundreds of thousands of hits on his videos and had been receiving royalties over the last year and a half in excessive of two hundred thousand dollars.

It was becoming quite clear what had been taking place in the basement suite along with the financial benefits. The problem was the people involved were now dead or missing. It would be difficult to convict people without more information and actual statements. It was easy to see how at least three people would end up dead, but not as easy to tell exactly who would benefit from it. It's possible it was revenge from one of the victims or the victim's family. There were numerous stories going around within the Indian community that there was some sort of extortion attempt made against the rapists that have not been paid. Most likely from another Indian gang that was aware of what was going on. In the following months there were numerous drive-by shootings and the two revenge killings. One of the stranger videos to have been downloaded to the same website by Parm was that of three elderly East Indian men standing in a small shed lined up behind a very familiar looking goat standing on a box. The men were seen to have their pants down. By chance one of the detectives on duty that night was shown the video. As strange as it sounds the goat looked very familiar. Detective

Polson pulled out his phone and browsed through the photos of the goat in the shed that he had taken that night. It appeared to be the same goat, also the box it was standing on in the same shed. After 25 years of Investigations on two different police departments this was definitely the first. The men in the video each taking their turn having their way with that cute friendly goat. Oddly enough the goat didn't seem to mind at all. The men were talking and laughing with a bottle of Crown Royal being passed among them. There were 30,000 hits and uploads just for that one video. It was surprising to all how many people took an interest in that sort of thing. Particularly from Middle Eastern countries.

Detective Paulson went back to the house with the SPCA expecting to seize the goat as evidence. Unfortunately, the goat was no longer there. The detective considered his options of putting a notice in the local paper as to the whereabouts of the missing goat. He also printed out a picture from his phone of the goat and contacted the landlord of the house. The landlord had no idea what had happened to the goat but suggested for one hundred and twenty dollars he could probably pick one up at the auction, laughing as he gave the suggestion to Detective Paulson. The investigation into the goat was discontinued. But is now a legend within the police department and a few individuals within the community.

The autopsy conducted on the three murder

victims turned up some oddities, one being efficiency of the two headshots by the same gun on the first two victims. It indicated the shooter was standing just inside the doorway of the bedroom. The two shots would have had to have been almost instantaneous. Neither Steve nor Harp had time to react. These would have been done by a person with years of experience and the ability to calmly walk into a room without notice. The shooter would have had to have gotten within five feet of them before taking the first shot. Hitting the head center mass then swinging 30 degrees for the second shot in less than half a second.

The third deceased male who had been identified through Interpol as a suspect in human trafficking and numerous murders in India was the most unusual case. Without any sign of offenses or defensive wounds he had been killed by a long symmetrical object pushed into his brain just below the bottom backside of a skull in an upward direction. It then appeared the object was swizzle around, liquifying 10% of the brain. Khon was found with a Smith & Wesson semi-auto that had been fired 5 times, then had jammed on the 6th round. His hands were gripped around an unusual looking dagger. It's suspected that at least two people possibly three had been involved in the murders. All though no evidence had been found linking a person or group to the crime.

Another East Indian gang had been accused

of the killings. The police were not positive of the other gang's involvement, however. It seemed more likely that these killings were some sort of retribution for the rapes that had been going on for the last year and a half.

CHAPTER 18

Janice and the techs on the team. had begun the rumor mills online, both threatening and accusing individuals of the crimes and murders. Drive by shooting along with bodies found shot inside of cars became common monthly events. She was still mad at Max for almost getting himself killed but her anger didn't last long. He was still her on the side guy and she wasn't about to bail on anyone. She considered the work she had done on this assignment to be some of her finest. Her ability to send and receive text and phone calls disguised as other people's IP addresses was cutting edge. She'd begun to understand multiple uses of the software that Sam had shared with them on a USB stick before his death.

Max was now enjoying a few months off. During that time, he had taken the old BMW on dozens off-road day trips up into the mountains along decommissioned logging roads. He always found it odd that you could come up to animals on a motorcycle and they would barely react. At times they would just sit still on the side of the road, such as the time a full-grown lynx crossed in front of him. Stopping for a few seconds in the middle of the road to observe him, then continuing off to the other side. On one occasion he came across a bear eating what looked like a small dead deer in the middle of the road. He tried waving at it and honking his horn, but the bear just went back to having his lunch with little more than a glance upward in his direction. On this trip the road was a single-laned with dense forest on either side. After a five- or ten-minute standoff Max turned around and found another route. No sense messing with a thin bear after a long winter. Max never felt more alive than when he was traveling on a deserted back road up in the mountains. On these trips, the only sound to be heard was the rumble of the motorcycle engine. The intoxicating smell of Maple or Douglas fir along with musty moss added to the enjoyment for Max. With just a slight increase in speed all thought of the city life would disappear from his mind. That small increase forces the exertion of one hundred percent of your mind, leaving no room for it to wander, considering alternate realities. Focusing on the here and now second by second.

He had pulled over at a natural bend in the road for a cup of tea, out of this fateful old tin thermos. Sipping on the tea and eating few crackers with some aged cheddar. He considered the old woman Elizabeth. What was his relationship with her and why are they connected? Dana had been bugging him for two months for a detailed explanation. Max wasn't even sure he himself, understood what she was. He decided then to take another trip to the coffee shop, or through the portals to the multiple dimensions if it was still active. The thought of spending months or years in an alternate reality where time does not exist concerned him. He felt more distant and detached from the people he cared about in this life each time he entered into it. He was changing by each experience, each time he had been exposed to the portal. Taking Dana into the portal would solve the problem of having to explain it to him. Possibly meeting Elizabeth there and let the cards fall where they lay, hmm... let her do the explanation and possibly get some answers for myself he thought.

The ride out of the mountains was smooth and serene. A warmth had come over me. I was one with the motorcycle. Gliding through the hills and curves. Perfect balance powering up the hills and out of curves, using the engine compression on the way down. Time felt like it was standing still. I had become the wind.

Max contacted Dana with the time and date for them to meet. They met at a non-descript parking area along an overpass by the freeway. Max explained that they would drive together from there and that it was another twenty minutes away. Dana continue to ask questions but was rebuffed with an explanation that, it would be easier and more believable for him to see and experience what he was asking about. It was one of those clear autumn days when the leaves were changing color on the trees. You could almost smell the change of seasons in the air. There was a little small talk in the truck on the way to the restaurant. Max had asked Dana if he had read the file regarding portals that Sam have given him on the USB stick. He said he had, but thought it was a little far-fetched, questioning what that had to do with the woman named Elizabeth. Max trying to sound as pragmatic as possible just said, that they're related, and it exists.

They pulled up to the small unassuming restaurant on the back-country road. As usual the hand painted sign in the window said open, there were no other cars in the parking lot. They entered and as usual there was half a dozen tables. On this occasion, two people sat at one and three at another. Max sat down at a table for two by the window, the other groups were both visible from the table. The same waitress as always came up with a cheerful, "how you boys doing, what can I get ya", with a smile. As usual I replied, "two coffees and two pieces of your homemade blueberry pie". Dana looked at me and said," I would have liked to have seen a menu" I said: there's only two things on the menu and it never changes". The coffee and pie arrive quickly as usual. Dana lifted it up to take a sip and commented, how did they know to put cream in it. I said that it wasn't coffee and there's no cream in it. He put the cup back down and started giving me that look, like, what the fucks with you. I then told him to slow down his breathing both in and out. On the outward breath expel no more air then you would need to blow out a candle, at the same time focusing on your diaphragm as you exhale. Look back down at your coffee, but not at it, through it. Not focusing your eyes on any given point. Dana followed the instructions exactly. I then heard a small gasp from him. Dana picked up what was no longer a coffee cup but a controlling device similar to a TV remote but round and half circular with no moving parts on it. Dana thought it odd that he seemed to know how to operate it. As for his homemade blueberry pie it just disappeared, with some regret. He began asking what the device was and what it was used for. Before the explanation, Max asked him to look at the other people in the restaurant. Then using the same breathing technique, focusing again on his diaphragm well he watched them. Within a few seconds there was another gasp from Dana, along with what the fuck he said. Max went directly into his prepared explanation that the portal was real, furthermore, the portal was actually a meeting and education platform within space and time for multiple species. Some of the species will communicate with you just through thought, so watch what you think. Others will communicate with a variety of sounds that will be instantaneously translated into our language whatever that is. Some of the species like ourselves have only been using the portal for a few thousand years. Other species much longer. These species are located in numerous locations on individual planets throughout the Solar System and the Galaxy.

To Max it was still unclear whether the physical body or just the consciousness was transported to this platform. It seemed very unlikely that the habitat for these different species would all be the same. He suspected that the physical bodies themselves stayed exactly where they were on whatever planet they came from. But the consciousness of the mind was recreated in another body in this location to allow it to interact with other species and gave it access to information. That might explain why very little emotion was experienced in this location. He believed the ancient part of our minds such as the fear and anger along with survival instincts were left behind. All the beings he'd been in contact with appear to base their interactions on logic and a similar rational thought process as himself. He suspected the creators of this technology were familiar with most of the life forms throughout the universe. Thousands, possibly millions of years more advanced than the current species interacting here. Max couldn't help but notice Dana was staring at species K 57. They were the plant species with very shapely dimensions. Before they got into discussing Elizabeth, he thought it would be entertaining to introduce Dana to them. He clearly recalled his first time interacting with K 57 with a smile on his face.

Dana walked up to the table like a kid approaching the best-looking girl in the school yard. He introduced himself and they, being a polite and charming species, began flirting with him. They communicate telepathically with a romantic grasp of the language. As usual they released hormones through the flower buds on their heads. Dana wasn't sure what was happening during the conversation, but he noticed he was getting an erection. A few seconds later feeling somewhat embarrassed as he had ejaculated in his pants. For the life of him he could not understand his sexual attraction to these plant-based species. The two K 57 species pointed towards the wet spot on his jeans giggling away. They suggested he come back later for seconds. Dana shuffle back to the table with his head somewhat lowered and shaking side to side. This had never happened to him before, he wasn't sure what was going on but was looking forward to meeting them again.

Max after having a similar experience years ago had taken the time to research their history. It turns out the plants have evolved both naturally and through genetic manipulation over thousands of years. In their original state they were not mobile except when moving through the wind, ocean, seas or rivers. They had evolved along with more advanced species hundreds of thousands of years ago. Initially they were just considered food by other species. They could survive in the harshest conditions even after being eaten, digested and disposed of. Their seeds could be frozen, thawed or buried for thousands of years only to come back as complete plants when conditions permitted. Several hundred thousand years ago a botanist of an advanced species took an interest in them. He soon realized that they were able to communicate with each other much more than ever suspected. He genetically altered the plant allowing them to move on hard surfaces with root like legs. He also added willowy arms to allow them to perform more advanced movement and operation of equipment. Within another hundred years they had become sanctioned beings. The drawback being some forms of foreign species still liked to eat them, considering them nothing more than a fruit or vegetable. They were able to regenerate quickly and typically held no hostility towards other species for their acts. Even when completely consumed, traces of them would be washed back into the creeks, rivers and oceans only to reproduce. The species was able to transmit telepathically all known knowledge and information to one another without the use of devices. Another problem that arose was that the pheromones they put off when interacting with other species cause a sexual reaction. On one planet they had been used in homes bedrooms and brothels as aphrodisiac to stimulate the sexual desires of other species. For the most part, the K 57 were quite content with this but through the implementation of common laws and rights given to all sanctioned beings, it was required to be done with consent.

To get around this, some of the species isolated them in homes then had their arms and legs clipped on a regular basis. This restricted their ability to move about freely. At some point in history several hundred years ago there was a small rebellion. A small portion of their species began to refuse to release pheromones. Within a few decades these few remaining rebels had been tossed out of the homes, office building and brothels usually ending up in a backyard or green area to fend for themselves. Well the grass is not always greener, and they began to miss the interactions with the other species. One of the older wiser plants had come to the conclusion that to coexist with other species they would need to accept some of the drawbacks. Such as the pets of other species that would often urinate on them or rub on them until there was nothing left but a stub sticking out of the soil. There was one species in particular on one planet with large antlers that used these plants to scrape the felt off their antlers several times a year. It left them covered with hair and dried blood, sometimes up to a week or two before it was washed off.

Dana was intrigued by the story Max was telling him, but still wanted to know about the old woman Elizabeth. He wasn't sure what to think at this point. It was a lot of information to process and he hadn't even gotten to the woman who had saved Max's life, Elizabeth, the one with the knitting needle. Max began thinking about where he would start. Out of the corner of his eye he thought he noticed a shimmer or some sort of movement, it appeared to be a distorted shape moving towards them and taking on more shape as it did so. It was the old woman Elizabeth. She walked up to the table dragging a chair with her, with a pointed finger she said, "I heard through the grapevine that you two boys we're looking for some answers". Needless to say, Both Max and Dana were surprised by her appearance.

And so, her story began. She started her life a few hundred years ago on a planet very similar to Earth, in a time that we would describe as the Middle Ages. Passing herself off as a man, she had fought side-by-side with the freemasons in the Holy Wars. All persons in known lands at the time had admitted defeat or had been killed. Most of the farmers or artisans had little interest in religion. They were more than happy to just replace their pagan idols and worship whatever name was chosen. Most noting that the fields still needed to be plowed and seeded whomever they worshipped.

She settled herself down in a village of what is now known to be in the country of Iraq. Her intent was to lead a quiet life and study the scriptures of the ancient scholars. She came across one book in particular that stirred her imagination and her soul for the search of the unknown. It described entities that could only be seen or communicated with after years of meditation and study. They were what would be considered today to be interdimensional. These entities were able to travel between worlds or planets that resonated at slightly different vibration frequencies. They also understood and had access to two portals such as this one. On every planet there were meridians and intersecting lines that enhanced the entities ability to change their vibration. With practice and training most advanced species were able to interact on different planes of existence. The first time Elizabeth encountered one of these beings, she was somewhat surprised that it was half her size. The entity immediately began waving its arms demanding that she bow to her God. Instead of bowing, she drew her sword and advised the entity to explain itself or have its head removed. With very little delay or encouragement the entity named Nocca explained the truth behind what he was, which was a more technically advanced culture. Elizabeth questioned Nocca as to the other teachings in the book she had read. Nocca agreed to teach Elizabeth about the book and his species if she could guarantee his safety in the small village. An agreement was made. For forty years Nocca trained Elizabeth and three generations of children and young adults in mathematics, astronomy, engineering, agriculture and medicine. Elizabeth was getting old and it was time for Nocca to leave. With one last gesture Nocca gave Elizabeth the spice of the immortals. She would now age very slowly and regain the strength of her youth. She could still be killed but it would be difficult.

With prosperity in her new homeland she began to recall the original teachings from the book. She was now the gardener described in legend. She would spend the rest of her years for centuries weeding the garden on the different planets that she could travel to. She understood tyranny and evil needed to be controlled. If left unattended it would destroy communities, countries and the planets. Elizabeth explained to Max and Dana that she did not know exactly how she knew where and when to be. She believed it had something to do with her teachings or meditations, or possibly the spice she had been given by Nocca.

What appeared before Elizabeth during her meditations was fine web-like lines running through all directions, beyond the sky and the horizons, through herself and the earth or planet that she was on. An infinite number of fine lines. They displayed slightly different colours and thickness but most importantly there was a vibration for each entity. Also, the intensity of the colors. She seemed to be able to see both the lines up close to her and far away, always shimmering. If she looked over head and around herself, she would notice a pitch that was slightly off, sometimes close by, other times light years away. By focusing her mind towards that single pitch, she was able to identify its location. Then by focusing her attention on the single entity that was out of tune she could transport herself to the exact location by matching its vibration. This allowed her to travel through time & space instantaneously. That was how she was able to appear at the exact time when she was needed or perhaps just to give assistance to problems before they escalated. Immediately after the encounter she would return to our normal vibration which would return her to her home planet. Some of the vibrations were much brighter and stronger than others such as Max's and Dana's and her good friend Sam's before his passing. She and others like her were considered gardeners in the universe. Groups such as the collectors that Max, Dana and the others belonged to were considered farmers of an individual planet. Pruning and weeding the garden on a local level.

Elizabeth used Khon as an example, as a child he was slightly out of tune but had not acted on it. At best he would have had a miserable life with proper guidance. His natural tendency was to become a monster. On an unconscious level taking the lives of others would give him hope that their energy would somehow move into him. The people around him would know something was different but not understand it. Possibly mistaking it for a sign of him being unique rather than defective. He would have never been able to feel the normal emotions or understand the connections of family, friends or countrymen we take for granted. Any connection between Khon and another individual would have ended in the death of one of them.

People of a high vibrational level can be seen with training. Like the members recruited into the collectors. Elizabeth's advice was to continue training in the meditations. As for now she had some nasty business to take care of. She began to blur, then went out of focus and disappeared. Dana mumbled, "that's not quite what I was expecting". Yeah, Max agreed, he had heard Sam referred to the group as farmers, but Max had not jumped to the conclusion that it had a literal meaning. "I thought it more a metaphorical expression. I always thought of it as, washing shit off the sidewalk, I used to say, more like the job of a caretaker. Who would have known there's some sort of cosmic connection? I need a damn drink, or two. How about you Dana"?

CHAPTER 19

The ride back to my house was a quiet one. Processing what we have been told by Elizabeth reached into the depths of our souls. I thought it one point I was going to have to pull over on the side of the road to throw up. I calmed my breathing down with the meditation techniques I have been encouraged to practice. The wife and kids were out of the house for the weekend. Dana and I sat out on the deck with the westerly view watching the late summer sun hanging just over the horizon. Along with a forty-ounce bottle of bourbon and a couple of Cuban Cohibas. While sipping the first three or four drinks we were both pretty quiet. Then there was the odd, what the hell have we gotten ourselves into? Things seemed a lot simpler a few days ago. I could hear Dana controlling his intake and exhale of air through his mouth as I had been doing for the last hour starting back in the truck.

I'm not sure which of us noticed it first, but I started seeing thin lines like strands of a web out in the horizon. They were coming in and out of focus and appeared to be of different colors and intensity. I was wondering if it was the bourbon having some effect on me when my ears popped a couple of times. As if I had jumped into a deep pool or was changing altitude in an unpressurized plane. I thought I could hear a slight ringing in my ears, but that's not what this was. It was something else more like tones from a harp off in the distance. I turned towards Dana and asked if he could see the lines. He turned towards me, also nodded then went back to looking out over the horizon. I began focusing on individual lines and the different vibrations there were a few clusters off in the distance that sounded to be out of tune. There were three or four locations in China and a couple in India. I had no idea how I instinctively knew their locations. I thought it was something I would have to look into. The lines disappeared off into the distance after about an hour or so along with most of the Bourbon.

That was enough for me for one day. I headed off to bed knowing Dana would let himself out.

I woke up with my wife snuggled under my arm, head leaning on my chest, except it wasn't. It was Rosie, our blue heeler bitch who had taken to jumping into bed with me whenever my wife isn't around. I think she thought she was my girlfriend. "Rosie what are you doing in my bed'? Tilting her head down, she would pretend she didn't know how she got there. "Rosie, you're not supposed to be on the bed". There would then be a little whining and an attempt to lick my face. Apparently, she just wanted someone to scratch her belly. Okay I gave in;

now get off the bed. She then spent the rest of the morning following me round hoping for a piece of sausage to fall on the floor.

I contacted Chan, our research and tech guy, in the morning, hoping he could figure out some sort of relationship or answers to what I had seen. What was the relationship between the Shanghai Nuclear plant, the metal foundry and the shipping docks? There were the strong clusters or groups in each area out of tune as Elisabeth had described. He, Chan had gotten back to me and said it would take a few weeks. He still had contacts in mainland China. What he didn't say was that there was a large network of spies in government, industry and technologies that worked both sides of the street. Money was their only God in the one child families. Fifty years of only single child families had produced generations of people who cared about nothing but themselves. Always spoiled and catered to by two parents had created a world that only revolves around themselves.

With a population of 1.2 billion it wasn't hard to hide things when you spread money around. If money wasn't enough of an incentive, then any persons not falling in line_were threatened. Both their livelihood and their families. What Chan was getting whispers of, was that the spent uranium rods from the nuclear reactors that were supposed to be going into deep underground storage in central China weren't. The rods were being cut into small pieces and added to large vats of molten steel used to make rebar. They were then sprayed with what was supposed to be a rust inhibitor, but in fact just prevented detection of radioactive material for several years. The rebar was then shipped overseas to foreign countries throughout the world at a discounted price to be used in construction. North America being one of their larger markets had begun to notice some abnormalities. Some of the anomalies over the last ten years were that concrete foundations, walls and columns were now generating heat. In some of the larger commercial projects electrical currents were being produced within the rebar along with deterioration and fracking of the concrete. The only way for rebar to produce heat is if Uranium was mixed into the metal at the foundry and was now releasing the isotopes.

At some levels of government, notice was being taken. Gag orders were in place for the last ten years for any government funded research. Safe radioactivity levels were increased by eight hundred percent. Gagger counters were now installed at most border crossings. Companies involved in major construction were advised to keep quiet if they ever wanted another contract. All was running smoothly.

There was a variety of players involved, upper management of the plaint, nuclear government bodies, floor workers on site shipping and receiving. On a few occasions China had advised smaller countries that hinted at what they suspected, that they should be more polite to a future world superpower under the guise of trade talks when questions had arisen regarding the origin of the rebar. Always claiming it was naturally occurring. Dozens of people had been murdered over the years or made to disappear. Of course, the outrage would be worldwide if the general public was to understand the implications. A slow poisoning of society by a foreign country.

Chan went methodically through the details, also the when, where and how the plutonium rods were being disposed of at the foundry by adding them to the vats of molten metal for rebar. He had lists of names, addresses, phone numbers, IP addresses, email addresses and access to their social media. There were hundreds of people involved and probably thousands that were aware of what was going on. The task was immense. It could possibly take years to plan and implement. On some cosmic level it was now quite obvious why they were strands and clusters of strands not in tune in China and we haven't even got to India yet.

CHAPTER 20

A few days after Chan have given the report to the group, he received a coded message. It was from his contacts within China. The group working within China thanked Chan for the information, then asked if he give them a few weeks to look after the situation themselves. Almost two weeks to the date there was a radiation leak at the main Nuclear Power Plant outside of Shanghai. The nuclear facility itself was not in danger but 85 people have died in the accident. A meeting was immediately called for all of the top nuclear advisors for this transportation and safety of plutonium rods. Several top-ranking officials were required to attend from the Chinese National Party. The meetings went on for several days at which time it was wound up with a tour of the facility. Security was tight and all the attendees were required to be transported by plane the next day. Unfortunately, there was a malfunction with the aircraft at 36,000 feet. The plane had lost power and control for no apparent reason. It crashed into a mountainside with a total loss of life. All 138 persons on board died.

It was a rare occasion when the Chinese national television stations reported instances such as this. With great sorrow they announced the unfortunate deaths of so many people. The names and faces were published of all the deceased. What it didn't say was that another thirty-five people had been arrested that were involved with the transportation or the melting of the rods at the refinery. Any family members that tried to find out the whereabouts of the people that were detained or arrested we're told that they were being re-educated and not to expect them back.

I was back on the sun deck at the end of the day of a long Indian summer. Dana had stopped by to check if there were any updates. I pulled out a bottle of bourbon and three short glasses. One for myself, one for Dana and one for Sam. Sam had been buried for six months now, but I still had some sort of feeling that he was involved in the shit that went down in China. The damn Blue Heeler had been following me around all day. Probably waiting for a sausage to fall out of my pocket. At least she'd stop staring at me and was happy with just lying on my feet. Dana was good company and as usual, always on the quiet side. Looking west towards the red dragon, I began to see the lines again. Then I could see wisps of shimmering webs radiating from the earth to the sky. I think I was seeing the update, along with Dana. The lines, as far as I could see were tuned to that harp-like sound that the universe pulsates to. There were always a few that needed to be looked at or adjusted but nothing like the clusters we had seen before. I wasn't sure what I was feeling. it felt like I had been left out, Chan was tight-lipped about who it cleaned up the problem. We all knew you couldn't repeat what you didn't know.

A few days later the story broke in a smaller newspaper. It outlined how an amateur investigator with a degree in physics had been finding unusual readings in foundations with his Geiger counter. He began contacting independent researchers and universities with the information. The articles were soon picked up by construction and technical magazines. This led to an independent investigation into the rebar shipped from China throughout the world, that had been used in construction. Numerous arrests were made along with the reimbursement and compensation for the faulty building materials.

It would appear for now that most of the smaller clusters in China were probably just individuals that needed to be cleaned up. As for the groups of smaller clusters in India, that would be for another day.

About the Author

Written by his son Brandon. My father, by profession is a semi retired commercial truck mechanic. He has loved listening to and telling stories throughout my life. As part of his profession he had written thousands of one line and single page descriptions of work-related repairs. Mostly true, some embellishment and a few lies. Can you believe that? A mechanic that lies about the work that was done and charged people for.

George Jobb has worked a variety of jobs since the age of 14; such as waiter, busser, cook, mill worker, diamond driller, plumber, truck driver, reserve soldier self employed, commercial truck mechanic, Truck shop owner, commercial diver, and skipper.

He has been a lifelong practitioner of martial arts with 25 years of amateur competitions. He holds a 3rd degree black belt in Judo. Sustaining such injuries; 6 dislocated shoulders, 3 broken ribs, 1 dislocated knee, 1 herniated disk, numerous broken toes and at one time had trouble wiping his own ass. Also, 1st kyu brown belt in Shotokan Karate, 3 years of Brazilian Jiu Jitsu and a year of amateur boxing from which he still admits he does not like being punched in the head, but who does? His highest level of competition was 3-time medalist at the World Judo Masters. Placing first in Tokyo Japan in the 100kg - 40 to 45-year-old division in 2003.

He has owned, fixed, bought and sold and ridden motorcycles since the age of 14 and still rides today.

Other Books and Articles Written by George Jobb

It All Started With A Few Rums, Available on Amazon

Numerous articles written for the Gringo Gazette located in Cabo San Lucas